UNTOUCHABLE WITCH

UNTOUCHABLE WITCH

SCHOOL OF NECESSARY MAGIC RAINE CAMPBELL™
BOOK 07

JUDITH BERENS   MARTHA CARR   MICHAEL ANDERLE

DISRUPTIVE IMAGINATION

LMBPN Publishing
PMB 196, 2540 South Maryland Pkwy
Las Vegas, NV 89109

First US edition, May 2019
Version 1.03, July 2020
Print ISBN: 978-1-64202-257-5

Thanks to the JIT Readers

Daniel Weigert
Misty Roa
Jeff Eaton
Nicole Emens
Diane L. Smith
Larry Omans
Micky Cocker
Peter Manis

If we've missed anyone, please let us know!

Editor
The Skyhunter Editing Team

DEDICATIONS

From Martha

To everyone who still believes in magic
and all the possibilities that holds.
To all the readers who make this
entire ride so much fun.
And to my son, Louie and so many wonderful friends who
remind me all the time of what
really matters and how wonderful
life can be in any given moment.

From Michael

To Family, Friends and
Those Who Love
To Read.
May We All Enjoy Grace
To Live The Life We Are
Called.

CHAPTER ONE

A slight breeze carried the briny scent of the sea to Raine where she rested her arms on the ferry's deck railing. The vessel continued its modest churn through the mostly smooth waters of the Gulf of Maine. She smiled when the experience triggered a memory of a summer ferry trip on Lake Michigan from years earlier, long before she ever suspected she would become part of the magical community.

The present relaxing jaunt from the mainland could have easily been mistaken for a tourist trip, but their real destination was a restricted island filled with magical creatures and plants. While it was an exciting location, their purpose was to help with an academic survey project.

She surveyed the horizon, looking for any sign of whales or large fish. Her ocean trip had given her many wonderful views of birds, but nothing else.

The heavily forested island sprawled in the distance, more a dark bump on the horizon than anything with discernible details for the moment. That they were able to see it meant, if Raine had performed the calculations correctly, they were about twenty to thirty minutes away from disembarking and beginning their first summer adventure with the School of Necessary Magic.

Not only was it the FBI Trouble Squad's first real excursion together outside the school curriculum, but the island research trip also represented a new effort for the school itself. The group of friends was helping to pioneer something totally new that might become a tradition for decades to come.

Raine's heart kicked up as a mixture of concern and excitement bubbled through her. Her summers were usually spent practicing magic and studying FBI material, and the change in her normal plan did raise a few questions. A few weeks prior, she had begun to worry that the trip might delay her entry into the FBI, but Agent Connor had assured her that a couple of months of not obsessing over all things agency-related wouldn't hurt her. He'd even suggested that they could spin it as a field training exercise given that it wasn't a normal zoological and botanical survey.

How many FBI agents could claim they'd spent months on an island filled with unusual magic beings?

Another gust blew a few strands of her light hair into her eyes. Someday, she'd have to take a long cruise around the world and appreciate all the wonders of Earth at a slow pace, rather than the sprint of the last several years. Learning she held magic had opened the door to so many wonderful experiences, and as much as she loved her school and friends there, she also increasingly understood that there was only so much she could learn from books and lectures. Even the Queen of the Library accepted that it represented only the beginning of wisdom.

Of course, the school managed to provide more than enough practical experiences, and every new adventure was exciting and stressful at the same time. She'd become so accustomed to being a witch at the School of Necessary Magic and an FBI trainee that the low-key summer project provided an almost startling contrast. They'd helped apprehend a chaos witch and learned about the birth of a unique magical being not all that many weeks prior, and that was merely another semester at the school. She might have gotten into trouble with her friends, but they always found a way out of it.

The entire FBI Trouble Squad was on the ferry, along with Professors Powell and Hudson. The magicals were the only passengers aboard, with the only other people being the Mainer crew operating out of Portland. Most of the other students and the professors sat inside the enclosed section of the passenger deck. They'd wearied of staring at the ocean after the first twenty minutes of their journey.

Sara smiled and walked up beside her. "You can't get enough, can you? It's only a stretch of water."

"It's not only a stretch of water. It's soothing."

The kitsune laughed. "Cameron doesn't agree."

"Is he doing okay?" Raine asked and sighed. "I would be inside, but he seemed annoyed when I tried to sit with him."

"He hasn't thrown up." Sara shrugged. "And of course, Mr. Overprotective doesn't want his girlfriend to watch him lose to water. We're all in there keeping an eye on him. Don't worry about it."

"That's good." She sighed and returned to staring at the ocean.

"Have you seen any whales?"

Raine shook her head. "No, but according to Professor Powell, we probably wouldn't see them anyway so close to the island because of the unusual magic. They might be repelled by it. I hoped he was wrong, but…" She shrugged.

"No whales?" The girl's smile turned into a playful grin. "What about any Kraken?"

"No. No Kraken, either." She laughed and pointed to the sky. A small flock of seagulls flapped toward the island. "Not everything's exotic and magical, I guess, even when you're talking about an island with heavy magic."

"You don't know that." Her friend shrugged. "For all you know, those seagulls can speak. Or even better, they sing and have a magical seagull band that performs seagull death metal."

"Seagull death metal? What does that sound like?"

"Lots of screeching. Like, you know, metal." Sara pointed to the birds. "You'll have to ask them."

"Maybe I will." Raine gestured toward an open door that accessed the seating area. "I'll head in. I should at least be with Cameron for the last few minutes. He might want to play all tough, but I don't want him to think I don't care."

The other girl nodded. "Let's go."

They wandered inside. The room was filled with plastic benches, and a smattering of bolted-down metal tables and chairs occupied the remainder of the passenger area. Narrow stairs descended to a vehicle area, but no cars rode the ferry that day. The other students and professors sat around chatting, their suitcases beside them.

Evie sat at a table with William and Professor Hudson. She sighed. "I still feel bad for Juniper and Malcolm. I know they both looked forward to this trip as much as we did."

Professor Hudson nodded. "It's unfortunate. Those two seem to have excessive bad luck at times. But I think it's best not to bring it up with them when they return to school because of the embarrassing nature of their respective incidents."

Neither of the professors had specifically detailed what happened to Juniper and Malcolm other than that it was "embarrassing" and related to magic. Raine and her friends had been polite enough not to inquire deeper.

"I still don't get one thing," William said with shrug. "I know it's not the end of the world that our school's only brought seven students, but why not simply choose two others? You had more than nine people on your list, right? It's not like we're the only students at the school, even if we do...get in trouble a lot."

Professor Hudson glanced at Professor Powell, her eyebrow raised in question. He leaned against a wall with his arms folded. He nodded to her with a knowing look.

"Taking a group of students on a magical research trip requires careful balancing of personalities and other factors, including general academic strengths and weaknesses." Professor Hudson smiled. "And while this isn't a trip lasting as long as one of your typical semesters, we were rather cognizant of a number of factors—including the aforementioned personality balance—when we selected the participants. Although there are other students who are compatible with this group, we didn't feel that including someone who already believed they would be included as a last-minute replacement would be conducive to the start of a good experience. Teacher's instinct, if you will."

William nodded. "That makes sense. I'm not complaining, as long as the Orono guys don't pull something."

Professor Powell laughed and stepped away from the wall. "The Orono Academy for Arcane Studies doesn't hold any particular animosity toward our school. If you're worried about Louper rivalries, don't be."

"Just saying." The half-Ifrit shrugged. "There are jerks, even at our school."

"True," Professor Hudson interjected, "but keep in mind that those students have also been selected for success and personality balance. The Orono professors have no more desire for bickering among students than we do."

Philip flashed a smile at Sara. "I don't care if we only have seven people. I'm excited. Even the name sounds so cool. The Magical Multitudes Project. I wanted my summer to be dedicated to some kind of service project, and this is a helpful one that also lets me have a cool adventure. Nice. I couldn't have asked for more."

"I'm glad you're enthusiastic, Philip," Professor Powell said, "but it is important to realize that this survey project won't always involve flashy and impressive animals. Not everything magical or from Oriceran is a dragon or unicorn. You might be annoyed after cataloging the tenth species of magical weed, and most of the animals on the island will be normal non-magical Earth animals. We don't have to catalog them as part of our project, but you'll see far more of them than the opposite."

The young wizard looked a little disappointed at the possibility, but Evie's breath caught at the mention of the weeds.

Adrien sat at a table on his own and looked out a window. "It never hurts to spend time in the wilderness, regardless of one's reasons. It's also good to break up one's routine. It helps when returning to training to identify ruts in your regimen, which can then be adjusted for maximum training efficiency."

Philip laughed. "Dude, not everything's about training."

The elf gave him a brief glance. "No, but it doesn't hurt to apply it to training if you can. All I'm trying to say is that I plan to enjoy my time here."

"I can't argue with that."

Raine felt bad for the elf. Everyone else on the trip conveniently had their significant other with them, but Christie hadn't been selected. Adrien hadn't complained about it at all, but it had to hurt him, at least a little. Even though the trip was mostly work and not a couple of months of unaccompanied beach fun, most of them were about to spend more summer time together than they normally did.

Evie rubbed her hands together. "I'm excited to see what kind of magical herbs might grow on the island. I know I probably won't be able to take any of them for potions, but it's still interesting. It'll help me practice my identification skills."

Professor Hudson gave her a sly smile. "I'm sure we can

work something out where you can take a few small samples."

Her eyes widened. "Really?"

The professor nodded. "As part of the project, we're not to significantly alter the island other than what's been done to set up the cabins and facilities at the camp. But I'm sure a few samples here and there won't be a problem—at least for the plants—provided they are known herbs. Unfortunately, the government restrictions mean they don't want any full plants or animals taken from the island until the survey is complete."

Raine frowned. "But birds fly back and forth. I saw some a minute ago." She gestured toward the roof.

Evie looked from her friend to the professor.

"It's less a quarantine than an effort to verify what actually lives on the island, but the plan is one they at least pay lip service to." Professor Hudson shrugged. "Don't worry too much. Think of it as camping with a little extra work. Don't pack any eggs, animals, or full plants, and you'll be fine."

Raine nodded and crossed toward a bench where Cameron lay. The boy was on his back, his face pale and his hand to his head. With a slightly darker shade of green, he might be able to blend in with a batch of cucumbers.

"How are you doing?" she asked.

"Still seasick," the shifter moaned. "I don't get it. I know I'm a shifter and I shouldn't be the one to say much, but we're going to a magical island to help catalog magical animals—and we've come from a magic school—so why couldn't we have used magic to get there? Or couldn't they have set up a Starbucks cart to make it really easy?"

Professor Powell maintained an easy smile and stepped away from the wall. "There's enough magical interference to not only affect electronics but also certain types of magic. Although basic spells work well enough, trying to open portals to New Firefly Island is a difficult proposition at best. There are other spells that can be helpful for transportation, but one concept we can reinforce during this trip is that there's a time and place for magic. Even on Oriceran, they don't use magic for everything. A brief ferry ride should be something every student of the School of Necessary Magic should be able to handle."

Cameron groaned and rolled to his side. "This isn't like having magic to tie my shoelaces or anything. I simply don't want to be sick."

"Fair enough." The professor nodded and retrieved his wand from his jacket. "I can do something to help with the seasickness."

"Please."

He spoke an incantation and followed with a few quick flicks of his wand. The tip glowed a dull blue. He placed it against Cameron's forehead, and the light disappeared.

The boy took a deep breath and exhaled slowly. He sat up and blinked but already looked more comfortable. "That helped. Thanks. I'll never join the Navy, though."

"I hope you get your sea legs sooner rather than later." A wicked grin reappeared on Professor Powell's face. "According to our friends from the Orono Academy for Arcane Studies, because of the dense forests, boats might be the best way to get around the island."

Cameron moaned and slumped miserably. His friends were polite enough not to laugh at him.

CHAPTER TWO

The ferry slowed to a stop alongside a long wooden dock that edged the rocky beach. A half-dozen rowboats floated on the opposite side, tied to the dock. Scattered wooden cabins stood farther up the beach beyond an uneven wall of piled rock. They had arrived at New Firefly Island.

"Just a reminder," Professor Powell announced as the metal unloading ramp extended toward the dock with a loud grinding noise. "There's no electricity here. The background interference is still being studied, so I hope none of you bothered to bring your phones or other gadgets. I know we told you not to, but we have also told you many things these last few years that you haven't listened to."

The students all exchanged glances and a few shrugged. No one had brought their phones.

"There are also no pixies here to provide your meals or towns to wander off to for a bite to eat," he continued. "But there are ingredients available, and they're preserved by spells from the OAAS professors. You're all advanced students of magic, so this is a good time to test how much you can free yourself of your dependence on technology using your own skills. We're not cleared to hunt here, but we are cleared to fish." He smiled. "You have an entire summer where you won't ever have to worry if you're doing too much with magic."

Philip frowned. "And what about showers?" He pointed at a long stretch of green-brown kelp. "Besides being salty, that's not exactly the place where I want to take a bath."

Professor Powell laughed. "Of course we don't expect you to go without bathing for two months. There are appropriate sources of water. From what I've been told, there's a well they dug using magic that will supply all our freshwater needs. It's also filtered." He looked at Professor Hudson, who gave him a slight nod in response. "We won't simply drop you into the woods and tell you to survive. The purpose of this trip is to expose you to a different school and utilize the skills you've learned to help with this survey project. This isn't a survival exercise."

Evie grimaced. "I would hope not."

Adrien looked slightly disappointed at the explanation.

The ramp clanked against the deck and the entire ferry shuddered. Raine all but sprinted toward the ramp, dragging her suitcase behind her. The island research trip might not be hunting criminals or studying case files, but it would still reinforce attention to detail. That was a useful FBI agent skill regardless of the nature of the investigation.

Cameron hurried after his girlfriend, chuckling and shaking his head. The other students filtered down the ramp, their faces communicating varying degrees of enthusiasm. No one looked worried or disappointed with the exception of Adrien. Professors Powell and Hudson brought up the rear.

A large, broad-shouldered man in long khaki shorts with a matching twill short-sleeved work shirt waited at the end of a long pier, a black wand hanging from his belt. A wide-brim straw hat rested on his head, along with a huge smile on his face.

"Welcome!" he all but shouted at the new arrivals, his arms spread wide. "Or should I say welcome to New Firefly Island."

He rushed toward Raine so quickly, she almost drew her wand on reflex. Professor Powell and Professor Hudson didn't seem perturbed so she forced herself to relax.

"Professor Basil Kaylis, Botany and Potions Professor, Orono Academy for the Arcane Studies. And you must be…" He squinted for a moment before he snapped his fingers. "Raine Campbell, I presume?" He thrust his hand out. "A pleasure to make your acquaintance, Raine. I've been told a lot about you."

She shook his hand and was pleased to note that he had a firm grip. "Yes, Professor. I'm Raine." She nodded to Cameron as he stepped to her side. "This is Cameron."

Professor Kaylis gave Cameron a double-handed shake. "Ah, yes, great to meet you, my boy. We don't have any shifters in our group. A little four-legged assistance might prove quite helpful. I don't trust too many fancy transfigurations given the background environment we'll work in, so it's nice to have someone who can change without relying on complicated spells."

Cameron shrugged. "Uh, sure. Whatever I can do to be helpful."

"To be clear, Eleanor—excuse me, Professor Hudson—has told me all about you fine students." The professor waved to the witch, who offered him a polite nod in response. "We used to work together a few decades back. Before everything magical became all boring and public." He sighed.

"I hope everything she said was good," Raine said with a grin.

"The FBI Trouble Squad, eh?" He grinned mischievously.

Professor Hudson exhaled a quiet sigh.

Raine laughed. "Some people call us that, yes, but don't worry, we like it."

Cameron grumbled under his breath. Adrien frowned, as did William. Sara, Evie, and Philip smiled. Maybe Raine liked it more than the others.

She shrugged. "We never look for trouble, but we also can't ignore it when people need help. That's why I think of it as a good thing."

Her friends' expressions changed and pride filtered onto their faces.

"Excellent." Professor Kaylis nodded so hard his hat bounced. "That's the kind of initiative and responsibility that makes you an excellent choice for this project. Our students are good, but I'm afraid they haven't gone through as many adventures—or the same type, I suppose. They've had their fair share. I hope you don't find them too boring." He winked.

"I'm sure I won't, Professor."

He rushed from student to student, shook their hand, and greeted them before he finally reached Xander and did the same. "And a pleasure to finally meet you in person, Xander."

Professor Powell smiled. "Likewise, Basil."

The Maine professor gestured to the cabins. They were arranged in a rough circle around a central sandy area. A large rock firepit sprawled in the center and wooden benches surrounded it. A few wooden tables stood off to the side.

"My students are out in the field right now, but we'll all at least share dinner, of course. I'm eager to see you two groups mingle." Professor Kaylis clapped his hands together. "I'm so looking forward to this."

Raine took a few deep breaths as she looked around. The intensity of magic she sensed had increased the closer they moved to the island, but now that she actually stood there, the magical pressure distracted her. The background magic at the school was always noticeable, but it usually felt more distant.

"Do you have many spells up?" Raine asked. "I sense a considerable amount of magic. It's like being near the gates of the school or in the kemana. In some ways, it's almost...I don't want to say worse, but it's more noticeable."

A grin slid over Professor Kaylis' face. "That high level of natural background magic is merely one of the many aspects of New Firefly Island that is being investigated, but our contribution to the Magical Multitudes Project doesn't include that. We're focused on a flora and fauna survey. Other teams will come—not during this summer, mind you—to contribute to our understanding. It's much like a general magical dampener, in addition to its effects on electronics. They can do some satellite surveys, but those are limited."

She frowned in confusion. "Magical dampener? What do you mean?" She looked at Professor Powell. "I thought we're supposed to use magic to compensate for other things—or the lack of them, I suppose."

"Yes, of course," the Maine professor replied. "It's not that the island is anti-magic, only that it's difficult to use scrying spells, communications spells, and that kind of thing. Most spells that don't have an immediate effect or aren't targeted right away are hard to accomplish." He gestured grandly toward the cabins. "But we don't need all that now, do we? We have what we need already, and it's nothing a little extra effort and travel won't solve."

Professor Powell pointed toward the dense line of trees that marked the end of their small slice of civilization. "I take it you haven't found any evidence that this place was purposefully hidden?"

Adrien narrowed his eyes and surveyed the trees as if he expected enemies or monsters to emerge at any moment. William and Evie also looked concerned. Sara looked more curious than anything else.

Professor Kaylis let out a hearty guffaw. "Ah, yes. I've heard that theory, but even though this is my first trip to the island with students, it's not my first trip here. And no, I've seen no evidence of that. Not every new discovery is a conspiracy, even when it comes to magic."

The students relaxed with the exception of Adrien, who cast a baleful glare into the forest.

"Is it really such a funny idea?" Raine looked thoughtful.

"It's no sillier than hidden kemanas or some of the other secret islands and forests out there. I read a book last week that highlighted all the above-ground places where magicals were hidden even before the gates started opening. It's weird to think there are entire places where normal people didn't go for centuries, if not thousands of years."

The professor shook a finger cheerfully and smiled. "You're right, Raine. It's not inherently silly, but we have to be careful to distinguish between the mere possibility of something and the truth of it. That's why we're here doing an old-fashioned survey." He rubbed his hands together eagerly. "Sometimes, it's fun to get your hands dirty, too. Magic is fantastic, but it can make some people lazy."

Professor Hudson advanced toward him. "And is there anything we need to be made aware of? I believe that in your last communication, you mentioned an uptick in earthquakes?"

"Woah," Philip said. "Earthquakes?" He looked at Sara with concern, but she seemed more excited than worried. "No one said anything about earthquakes to me."

"It's fine." Professor Kaylis waved a hand dismissively. "Their strength is well within what has been recorded on the island. None of them are major, and they haven't even damaged the cabins. I merely wanted you to be aware of them so as to not be surprised—at least any more surprised than you would otherwise be with a minor shake of the ground."

A cabin door creaked open, and a bald, stout blue-skinned woman with yellow eyes emerged from the structure. She wore a similar straw hat, khaki shorts, and shirt combo as Professor Kaylis, although she was several feet shorter. Her height made her taller than the typical gnome, but not by much.

The woman sprinted toward the new arrivals, her short legs pumping. She skidded to a stop. "The people from the School of Unnecessary Magic!" she declared, a rough, low quality to her voice. "Welcome."

Professor Kaylis laughed. "That's the School of *Necessary* Magic."

"That's what I said, Basil." The woman pointed at Raine and Cameron. "Evie and Philip? Correct?"

Raine looked at Professor Kaylis for direction. He nodded.

"I'm Raine. This is Cameron."

The other students all took turns to introduce themselves.

The woman squinted and nodded. "Oh, yes. I'll get it eventually." She squared her shoulders and took a deep breath. "I'm Professor Tarelli. I specialize in magical zoology."

"You mean cryptozoology," Professor Kaylis with a smirk.

The woman glared at him. "I hate that term. I don't know why the headmaster insists on using it. I swear it's simply to annoy me. It's a biased term from the anti-magic times." She raised her hand and the air shimmered for a moment. "Oh, that's better. It's so hot today."

Raine blinked. It was a beautiful day with a light breeze, the temperature probably in the low seventies at most. Not too hot, not too cold. Almost perfect. "Too hot?"

Professor Kaylis cleared his throat. "Have any of you met a Nyran before?"

The students shook their heads.

Professor Tarelli's mouth made an O. "I'm so used to my own students understanding. My people are from arctic regions on Oriceran. It's been a challenge to adjust to such a hot place as Maine, but I'm sure that in a few more years, I'll settle. Or I'll finally go to Antarctica and a proper climate." She shook a finger at them in a cheerful warning. "And I've heard a million jokes about my name sounding like pasta, so don't bother making them." She spun on her boot heel and headed back toward her cabin, throwing her hand up without looking back. "It'll take me a while to learn your names. Please don't be offended."

Professor Hudson smiled. "To be clear, Nyran only have one name. They consider multiple names too divisive among their own people. So, please refer to her as Professor Tarelli even though you'll hear us call her Tarelli."

"True," Professor Kaylis replied. "And she's not always the best when it comes to social niceties, but she means well." He pointed toward the cabins. "Why don't we get you settled in? You can relax for a while until the other students return."

Raine's smile widened as the diminutive professor entered her cabin. She'd been on the island for only a few minutes and had already expanded her knowledge. It would be a great summer.

CHAPTER THREE

With a wide yawn, Raine stepped out of the cabin she shared with Evie and Sara. They were nothing special—four wooden chests and beds with wooden racks to hang a few clothes—but at least she wasn't forced to sleep on the ground for two months. It might not be the School of Necessary Magic, but it was hardly roughing it either.

Sara and Evie stepped out behind her. A ring of light orbs surrounded the cabins to push back the darkness that had crawled in with the retreat of the sun.

She blinked a few times at the unfamiliar teens spread between a few tables around the firepit. A roaring fire now crackled in the center, and several long skewers of fish roasted over the blaze. No one had so much as knocked on her door to let her know the other students had returned.

"It looks like the Orono students," Sara said with a smile. "Let's go say hello."

The Charlottesville girls approached the tables and Raine offered the students a wave and a soft smile.

A tall, handsome dark-haired boy with pointed ears stood and bowed in a melodramatic fashion. "Good evening, ladies. Let me be the first to introduce myself. I'm Asher, a Wood Elf." He gestured toward two girls who sat on either side of him. "Heidi and Kelly, both witches."

The Orono girls waved and offered a simultaneous, "Hey."

Raine waved back. "I'm Raine. I'm also a witch." She waited for her friends.

"Evie, also a witch. I'm really into potions."

An uncertain look passed over Sara's face. "Sara, kitsune."

A little anxious, Raine flicked her gaze from her friend to the Orono group. More than a few students had insulted her friend in their freshmen year. Not every magical believed other magicals deserved the same high-quality education.

"Kitsune?" Asher said with a wide grin. "Awesome. We don't have any at our school. That's real cool. I told everyone we were bound to meet some interesting students."

Relief erased the uncertainty on Sara's face.

Three other boys sat at another table.

"I'm Milo," explained a tall one. "I'm a wizard."

A muscular boy with light hair stood. "What's up? I'm Finn. I'm on our Louper team, but I won't hold that against you." He grinned and shrugged. "We're totally destroying you next year. Sorry."

Raine almost laughed, but she wasn't sure if it would be rude.

Finn nodded to another plain-looking boy, who looked

as uncomfortable as Sara had a few moments before. "This is Silas. He's also a wizard. He's quiet and shy so don't hold it against him. He's a cool guy when he decides to be."

A pretty girl with long brown hair stood from another table where she sat beside an Arpak girl. She squared her shoulders and raised her chain. A regal air hung about her. "I'm Josephine. I'm also a witch."

Her dark-skinned companion stood. Her feathered wings spread and an easy smile tilted her mouth. "Dnai. Nice to meet you all."

Evie looked at the students, a confused expression on her face. "Aren't there supposed to be nine of you?" She made a quick count and mouthed the numbers under her breath. "Where's the ninth student?"

"Oh, there was a family emergency for them at the last minute," Dnai said. She sighed and sat once more. "Too bad, too. But you know how it goes."

Raine nodded. "We lost a couple of people, to…uh, unexpected circumstances as well."

The Charlottesville boys appeared in the distance. They had taken a walk an hour before to explore the nearby beach. The rocky shoreline and churning water didn't appeal to Raine's sense of beach aesthetics, so she had turned them down.

She smiled and gestured toward the boys. "Time to meet the rest of our friends."

Twenty minutes and several more introductions later, the students all sat interspersed among the tables and munched on roasted fish and carrots. The professors remained in the cabins, perhaps to give the younger people a better chance to get to know each other. Professor Kaylis had popped out once, said nothing, and retreated into his cabin.

Raine swallowed a piece of fish. "This meal is a change of pace for us."

Asher, who sat beside her, offered her a dazzling smile. "So you don't eat a lot of fish at your school? Maybe you have someone making the food who is part fish and doesn't like the idea?"

She shook her head. "No, but we have pixies who do all our cooking. We show up, put in what we want—within limits—and it appears." She chuckled nervously. "It's all rather fancy compared to what I'm used to at home, but it feels weird to be on a school trip and not have the pixies providing the food."

Asher's eyebrows raised. "Really? Pixies, huh?"

Cameron looked at the Wood Elf from the other side of Raine. "You don't do it like that in Orono?" he asked

The elf shook his head regretfully. "Nope, no pixies. Students have to help with all the cooking. The professors take turns leading them. They are really into us doing everything together. Learn as a school, fail as a school. That's practically our motto." He leaned forward and lowered his voice. "Fortunately, they don't let all the professors do it. Professor Kaylis is...not good at it. We were lucky to have people who were good at healing magic ready when he did do it."

Everyone shared a laugh.

Raine glanced at her fish, her expression thoughtful.

"Huh. I never thought much about how other magic schools do things. Since the School of Necessary Magic was also basically my introduction to magical society, it's hard to remember at times that it's a single school with a single philosophy. I can see the advantages of having the students help with the cooking."

Evie smiled from across the table. "I'd love it if we did that at our school." She smiled at Asher. "I cook with the pixies all the time, but that's only because I'm into baking. It's not really part of our mealtimes."

William frowned. "I wouldn't want to have to do that. We have enough on our plate."

Josephine cleared her throat delicately. "It's like Asher said. At Orono, we work closely with the professors. It's almost like...an apprenticeship model in some ways, I suppose you could say." Her cheeks reddened. "I'm not trying to say anything's wrong with the way your school does things. It's different, that's all, and I can understand how it might seem weird."

Raine plopped a tiny roasted carrot into her mouth, chewed, and swallowed. "I'm sure there are many good ways to train students—"

Asher bolted from his seat and distracted her.

She blinked and stared at him in confusion. Cameron pushed hurriedly from the table and his quick gaze searched the area for threats. Adrien was up a second later, his hand in the air as if he was ready to summon a sword.

A little bewildered, Asher frowned at the tense boys before he seemed to realize what his action had caused. "Oh, sorry." He waved a hand. "Nothing bad. There's something you all should see. I almost forgot about it because I've already been here several days and everything seems less cool when you see it enough times for it to become familiar." He nodded to his fellow students. "Kill the lights."

The orbs winked out of existence one by one as the Orono students canceled the spells. A quick spell by Josephine quenched the fire with a splash of water and the remaining smoke drifted into the air. Stars filled the sky above them, clear and crisp in the darkness with the light pollution of cities a distant concern.

"The stars are pretty," Raine said. "But we have great views of the stars at our school." She shrugged and hoped they weren't too disappointed by the reaction.

"Not stars. They would be boring." Asher grinned and pointed behind her.

She turned and gasped.

Blue. Green. Red. Yellow. Purple. White. Dot after dot winked into existence and disappeared.

Raine tilted her head and squinted into the darkness. "Are those...fireflies?"

He sidled up behind her, his teeth barely visible in the darkness. "Yes. They're all sorts of colors on the island, but they won't go anywhere near our lights. I thought you should see them."

The frequency of the colorful glimmers increased to produce an eerily beautiful kaleidoscopic display. Small repeating patterns developed, almost like a careful language or code. Raine wasn't sure if it was coincidence or something fundamental to the display.

Evie gasped. "It's so pretty."

"It's almost hypnotic," William suggested. He blinked a

few times. "It's like they're watching us as much as we're watching them."

Adrien harrumphed almost as if he was disappointed that there was no danger. "I've seen nicer."

Sara laughed and nudged him with her elbow. "Don't be that way, Adrien. It's nice." She smiled at Asher. "Thanks for showing us this."

"Yeah, dude," Philip said. "It's actually cool. Don't be a downer."

Adrien shrugged but didn't offer another retort.

Josephine stood and walked toward the fireflies. The darkness concealed her features, but the outline of her movement was distinctive. There was something elegant and graceful about her manner. "If we're lucky, they might also do something even more special. Everyone needs to be totally silent for a little while, though, if you want to hear it."

Raine took a deep breath and nodded. The trees surrounding the campsite weren't anything special, and although they'd noticed a few unusually colorful birds earlier, the fireflies were their first direct experience with something on the island that didn't seem like anything they could find anywhere else in the country, let alone the planet.

The other students turned toward the forest and waited, the sound of their shallow breathing undetectable above the quiet moan of the wind and the swaying of the trees. Nature had retaken the island's soundscape for a few moments.

A high-pitched note sounded and resonated like a distant bell. A lower chime joined it and was rapidly followed by others. Soon, a symphony of overlapping melodies and harmonies played, like competing bell ensembles. Somehow, despite wide ranges of notes and chimes, no dissonance marred the music.

The students stood in silence and let the nighttime symphonies wash over them for several minutes.

The creak of a cabin door ended the music. The fireflies returned to their rainbow flashing.

Professor Tarelli stepped out of her cabin and sighed. "Oh, they are so sensitive," she called apologetically. "I'm sorry, but it's so exciting." She jogged toward the students, a small, faint shadow in the darkness but seemed to have no problem navigating without light. "Basil should teach you a thermographic vision spell or something of that nature. There are subtle changes even among the temperatures."

"Do you use a spell like that?" Raine asked.

"No. I partially see that way naturally." Professor Tarelli took a deep breath. "These kinds of creatures are one of the reasons I was so excited to be involved with this project, and all you students should be too. I don't think you fully appreciate what a wonderful opportunity you have this summer. The glories of magical knowledge will be visited upon you if you keep your mind open to the possibilities."

Raine's gaze darted to her finger where she wore her invisible True Cardinals ring. The professor's speech reminded her a little of the secret society's credo.

Asher groaned quietly, as did several other Orono students. Josephine, noticeably, did not. Raine suspected they had heard this speech several times.

"Several of the species identified here have only previously been found on Oriceran." Professor Tarelli gestured widely, an excited shadow in the darkness. "And there's no evidence of an active portal anywhere on the island, despite the high levels of magic. If anything, there's evidence that it would be difficult, if not impossible, to create one. So that raises a number of questions. Where did these species come from? If it was a small number, that would be one thing. We could say they came through a portal in the past when the situation was different and simply flourished in the absence of competition, but the more we search, the more we find. An entire near-Oriceran ecosystem exists on an island off the coast of Maine. That can't mean a few species sneaking through the occasional portal, especially when it's so hard to form one."

"Are you sure this isn't some...well, some magical pirate island?" Philip asked with a shrug. "Maybe they set a portal up away from the island and come over to it."

The professor shook her head. "There's been no evidence of any sapient species on the island. No artifacts, magical or otherwise. I—"

Raine's knees buckled as the ground shook and Cameron's arm immediately braced her. The tremor lasted only a few seconds, but it was more than enough to turn her stomach. It had been a long time since she'd last felt an earthquake.

The other professors all emerged from the cabins, their wands in hand.

"No light," Professor Tarelli shouted. "The students are watching the fireflies."

"Is everyone all right?" Professor Hudson called.

"They're all fine," the Nyran said with a wave of her hand. "We were discussing things. The glories of knowledge. The brilliance of learning. The earthquake is only more proof of that."

"Proof?" Raine asked.

"These earthquakes are inconsistent with the tectonic activity of this area, suggesting a magical origin, even if we've yet to feel a particular magical signature associated with them. Perhaps I'm wrong and there's a hidden portal deep in the heart of this island. We've yet to find it or identify the cause, although it's not our responsibility, but here we stand, on the cusp of pure discovery." She pointed at Raine. "Don't you agree, Sara?"

"I'm Raine." She chuckled and wondered if the Nyran professor had trouble with names as part of her personality or with telling people apart because of how her sight worked.

"Of course, of course."

Raine returned her gaze to the fireflies. She had already attended three years at the School of Necessary Magic, and every day, she learned something new. Her upcoming senior year wouldn't be the end of her education, only the end of her first stage. If a seasoned professor could remain excited about new discoveries and knowledge, she still had a lot to look forward to in the future.

Someday, she might even solve a case by understanding the song of rare Oriceran fireflies.

"There's so much to learn," she murmured.

"It's no big deal," Cameron replied. "We'll figure it all out."

"I'm not complaining."

Asher laughed. "Oh, you sound like Heidi and Silas."

Heidi rolled her eyes.

"What can I say?" Raine replied. "I like learning."

She stood there in the darkness and a smile grew on her face. New friends and new knowledge. It was a good first night on the island.

CHAPTER FOUR

"Hide and seek?" Raine asked. Her tone came out far more dubious than she'd intended.

They sat around the rekindled fire, the only current source of light. The professors had retired for the night and encouraged the students to get to know one another. According to Professor Kaylis, they would be allowed to rest the following day, so there was no reason to hold back on, as he put it, "the glories of interschool bonding."

Silas had gone to sleep, but the other seven Orono students remained. They'd chatted for about an hour and a half about general features of their respective schools and a little about themselves when Asher suggested the new activity.

"Aren't we a little old for hide and seek?" Adrien asked with an incredulous look.

Asher gave Adrien and Raine a bright smile. "Call it something else then. Hunt and hide. It'll be fun. We do something like this for new freshman at our school. Basically, we pair up and have a friendly competition, but the twist that makes it interesting is that any and all magic is allowed except for direct tracking magic." He scoffed. "And that doesn't even work here, so we don't need that rule. We'll have a hunting team and hiding one."

"Pair up?" Cameron rubbed his chin. "I can see how this might be fun. I'm good when it comes to tracking."

"I could see the value as a training exercise." Adrien frowned as he considered the idea.

Philip laughed. "It's okay to simply have fun, dude, even if Christie isn't here."

Adrien scoffed.

"I think it's exciting," Evie said.

William nodded his agreement. He didn't smile, but he didn't look annoyed.

Asher held a finger up. "But half the point of us hanging out tonight is supposed to be us getting to know each other, so we can't be boring and pair off with someone from our own schools."

Cameron frowned. "We can't?"

The Orono elf pushed to his feet and gestured around the circle of students surrounding the firepit. "Of course not. That's pointless. I like my friends from my school, but I know them already." He grinned. "We're all sitting next to someone from another school on one side or another. We should pair up with whoever's closest to us and not from our school." He turned and smiled at Raine. "With an FBI trainee on my side, I can't lose."

Raine laughed. "I don't know about that, but it does sound fun when you describe it that way."

Cameron grunted before he drew a deep breath and nodded to Josephine nearby, who smiled. The other teams included Milo and William, Sara and Kelly, Evie and Dnai, Philip and Heidi, and Finn with Adrien.

"Two rounds," Asher said and looked even more pleased with himself than before. "That way, everyone has their chance to hunt and hide. I think the hiding team should have a five-minute head start. We'll set a twenty-minute time limit to find them."

"Five minutes?" Cameron frowned. "That's a big head start for an island in the middle of the night."

"Why do something if it's not a challenge?" The elf cast a quick light orb and tossed it from one hand to the other. "How about two hiding teams per round? That gives us ten people looking for four."

Adrien nodded and a hint of a smile finally appeared. "There's more than one way to track someone. I'm not worried."

Everyone nodded their agreement.

"Fine." Cameron folded his arms. "Who will hide first?"

Asher looked at Raine. "What do you say?"

"I'm game." She shrugged.

"What do you think?" Sara asked Kelly.

The witch nodded, an eager gleam in her eye. "Let's do this."

"Time to get hiding!" the Wood Elf shouted.

Five minutes later, Asher stood beside a tree. "This looks good." Small squares appeared and shifted across his body, changing color to match the shadows and the tree behind him. Only a small amount of stray light from the distant fire, stars, and moon seeped through his increasing camouflage.

"Is this why you wanted to play this game?" Raine asked.

"What can I say? I suggested a game I have a natural advantage at." Soon, the Wood Elf was gone and to see was nothing there but a tree.

She drew her wand and cast a quick stealth spell to render herself invisible. "This was one of the earlier spells I learned," she murmured quietly. "We needed it to sneak into the kemana."

"Sneak into the kemana? Why? Aren't you allowed to go?" He sounded surprised.

"Freshmen can't go." She chuckled. "Not that it stopped most of the freshmen at the school. I'm not sure if the rule is actually because the professors feel it's relevant, or if it's simply a test of initiative."

"Oh. We don't actually have a kemana at our school. There's one under Bar Harbor, but that's not exactly a place we can walk to without going to the Starbucks, so we have fewer opportunities to sneak into it." Asher snickered. "Back in the day, the whole balancing out your magic by taking trips to the kemana to recharge magic was a big part of the school's education. There are still many things there based around that, even though there's more magic now. Sure, there could be a lot more, but it's not like I sit around worrying about having enough magic to do stuff."

Raine hadn't realized how unsettling it could be to chat to someone you couldn't see. "I guess I don't always think about how lucky we are to have a kemana. We weren't allowed to even go into Charlottesville until this school year, so it would have been annoying if we were stuck at the school with both the kemana and the town off-limits."

The tree shimmered for a moment, which signaled a slight movement by Asher. "Oh, they don't restrict us. Our school isn't hidden like yours. They don't advertise it on the Internet, of course, but the school's been there a while, even if it being a purely magic school is a new thing. And there are many witches and wizards who already had roots in Orono. There is no big restriction on us going into town, and even though it's small, there are enough magicals to keep students in check if something goes wrong. From everything you told us earlier, it's a different vibe at our school. We're more laid back in some ways, but we don't have some of the cool stuff you have, either. Our school is smaller than yours, and we don't have as many clubs and things like that."

"I can't really say which is better," Raine said. She sucked in a breath at the sound of something scurrying nearby but released it in a puff of air when a fox padded past nearby and occasionally sniffed at the air. She waited until the animal had moved into the undergrowth before she continued. "I told you at dinner about how my magic came out when I confronted bullies and they sent me to the School of Necessary Magic. How did you end up at the Orono Academy for Arcane Studies?"

The shadows in front of the tree shifted again, but Asher's camouflage remained intact. "Several members of my family have gone there. It's been a tradition since way back. You see, originally—before the gates opened—the school was basically an elite boarding school for wealthy New Englanders. Really, it was a place where influential magical families from different backgrounds could send their kids and where they could mix with less risk. It wasn't a true magic school because of restrictions from people like the Griffins, but once the gates opened, it made total sense to convert it into an actual magic academy. Everyone locally who wasn't in the know always thought something was spooky about it anyway. I'm only the second in my family to go there since it officially changed into an open magic school."

Raine knelt and held her breath when some branches crunched under her knees. "Legacy, huh? That's like me in the FBI."

"True." The shadows flipped into Asher's face and he grinned before the camouflage returned. "Sometimes, I don't like going there because it's small. I wish I attended some huge normal non-magical high school or a place like yours."

"For more clubs?" she asked.

"More girls. If you and your friends are typical, I would really love to be in Charlottesville right now."

She might not be able to see Asher, but she could all but hear his grin.

"Um, okay." She coughed. "That's…uh, interesting."

"I'm not saying anything bad about the girls at my school or the ones on this trip, but at this point, they're more like my sisters than anything else." He chuckled. "And even they aren't as interesting as you are. You'll be an FBI agent in a couple of years. Or did I misunderstand what you said at dinner?"

"No, that's how it'll work out." She rubbed the back of her neck and glanced over her shoulder, half-hopeful that one of the hunter pairs would burst through the trees. There was little hope of that, by the looks of things. Even though she spoke quietly with Asher, other than the fox, they hadn't been disturbed at all.

Raine sighed heavily.

"What's wrong?" Asher asked.

"Look, Asher, I want to be clear with you." She stared at the tree where he remained camouflaged, an invisible girl talking to a concealed boy. "I'm in a relationship."

He groaned. "Let me guess. You're with Cameron?"

"Yes. How did you know?"

"I thought so. You had that vibe, but I also hoped I was wrong. Oh well. It doesn't hurt to ask, right?" His tone remained upbeat, to her surprise. "Forget I even mentioned anything. We still have a game to win, and I'm very competitive."

"That sounds good. Out of curiosity, is anyone in your group dating?"

The elf laughed. "Nope. I half-wonder if Professor Kaylis picked people who weren't together on purpose because he thought we would be too distracted by it. Wait." He barked out a laugh loud enough to send a nearby owl flying away from a tree in the distance. "Oops, sorry. Let me guess, everyone in your FBI Trouble Squad is together with someone?"

"Basically. Adrien's girlfriend's not on the trip. She's a senior."

"*That* guy has a girlfriend?"

Raine frowned. "He's a little stiff, but he's a good friend and a good person. He's like Silas. You simply have to get him to open up."

"Sorry." Asher's quiet snicker suggested he was not as sorry as he could be. "But he's really uptight. It's like that movie, *Manic Human Dream Girl*. Did you see that one?"

She couldn't help but laugh. "Yes, and I'll admit the movie did come up in discussion when Adrien first started dating his girlfriend."

A branch crackled in the distance and they both froze.

Asher blew out a quiet breath. "We should probably move," he whispered. "I'll switch to an invisibility spell instead of using my Wood Elf camo. We can have better mobility that way, even if both of us using spells might stand out more."

"Let's go." She licked her lips. He wasn't the only one who was competitive.

CHAPTER FIVE

Raine and Asher crept through the trees. The deeper into the forest they traveled, the more unusual the plants and animals became. Patches of glowing flowers provided muted illumination that allowed them to avoid using light orbs someone might notice from afar. A few plants twitched and shook in place, which made her question the distinction between a plant and an animal.

Owls, foxes, and mice patrolled the forest and four-legged birds with reflective eyes flew from branch to branch and emitted an occasional quiet squawk. She grimaced as a beetle the size of a rabbit scuttled in front of a glowing shrub. The soft light from the plant highlighted the metallic blue of its carapace.

"Ugh." She made a gagging sound. "That's disgusting."

"Oh, don't worry about those," her companion reassured her with a laugh. "We call them scuttlers, but according to Professor Tarelli, they're really helpful for aerating the soil and breaking down plant material. They mostly live underground. They only come out at night to eat."

She shuddered. "Are you telling me there are hungry giant beetles waiting under the ground?"

"Sure, but they won't go anywhere near a person. It's no big deal."

At a low growl nearby, the scuttler rushed away and disappeared into the darkened undergrowth.

Raine froze in place and pointed her wand into the forest. "Is this where you tell me you have big animals called growlers that don't bother people?"

"There's nothing dangerous this close to camp," Asher replied. "At least that we've seen." He sighed and dropped his invisibility, raised his hands, and squinted into the darkness. "And the professors let us wander into the woods without worrying too much, but I'll admit we haven't been out much farther than we are now."

She released her spell and cast a hasty shield. Being invisible might not be enough to stop an animal with acute hearing, and a creature on an island filled with unusual levels of magic might even be able to sense magic. It was important that she be able to see Asher if they had to fight together. She summoned a light orb.

The plants rustled in the distance and Raine's heart rate kicked up a notch. She reminded herself that it had to be safe and that Asher was right. There was no way the professors would let the students wander the island if it was dangerous. At least, that's how things would be managed at the School of Necessary Magic. But perhaps Professors Powell and Hudson had a different idea about testing people, and everything she'd learned about Orono suggested they might think challenging the students wasn't such a bad idea.

"Don't hurt it," the elf whispered. "No matter what it is, it might be endangered or even unique. We're here to catalog species, not kill them."

"I've had decent practice with restraining magic," she murmured in response.

The growling beast charged in the darkness. Raine pointed her wand, her jaw tight, ready to release a spell while she desperately hoped the creature wouldn't prove immune.

A familiar wolf burst from the undergrowth.

Raine threw her arm in front of Asher. "It's okay. I know him."

The Wood Elf raised an eyebrow and lowered his hands. "Oh, I see."

Cameron shifted into human form, a slight smirk on his face. "That was too easy."

She frowned at him but spun as she sensed magic behind her.

Josephine shimmered into existence, a soft smile on her face. "You were right, Cameron."

Asher threw his head back and groaned. "What happened? Did we talk too loudly?" He pointed at Josephine. "Or did you actually manage a tracking spell? If anyone could do it, it'd be you, Jo."

The witch shook her head lightly and nodded at Cameron. "He's the sole reason for our victory tonight. I would be lying if I claimed otherwise."

Raine twirled her wand in her fingers. "All that magic and it didn't help? Is he right? Did you hear us? I didn't want to sit there in silence in the dark for a half-hour." She gestured into the woods. "Especially with weird plants and giant beetles."

The other witch smiled. "The scuttlers are adorable in their own way."

"If you say so."

Cameron pointed at his nose. "I think I know my own girlfriend's scent by now."

Asher laughed. "Of course." He tapped his forehead. "That's me not thinking. I was so obsessed with merely hiding from everyone, I never even thought to try to hide my scent." He immediately looked thoughtful. "I don't even know a good spell for that, now that I think of it."

Raine shrugged. "I have a few ideas, but it's not something I've practiced."

The grin grew on her boyfriend's face. "This ended up as one of those lessons in flexibility that Professor Powell always talks about."

Something rushed through the undergrowth and flashes of red light cut through the shadows. Whatever or whoever the source of the noise and light seemed only about a dozen yards away.

The four students exchanged looks.

A grin grew on Asher's face. "We might as well help you find the next group."

Cameron frowned. "Maybe we should head back. I saw a lot of weird things on the way here."

"Stranger than a shifter, an elf, and two witches?"

He scoffed. "I'm only saying that the point of our trip is

to catalog stuff, and from what I heard, you guys didn't do any night surveys in the last few days."

"Yet." The elf shrugged. "But whatever. That has nothing to do with this." He summoned a light orb and rushed after the source of the noise. "What's life without a little adventure?" he shouted.

Raine jogged quickly to catch up to him.

"I think I've had enough adventure over the last few years." The shifter frowned and hurried after her.

Josephine laughed quietly before she fell in behind them.

The red lights dashed away from the group and their source disturbed the shrubs in its path.

Raine doubted that they were in pursuit of any students, but the dense foliage made it difficult to discern anything but shadows and red light.

"Spread out," Asher shouted. "Let's box them in!" He changed direction, as did Josephine.

The elf circled while Raine maintained her trajectory directly toward their quarry. Josephine pointed her wand down and chanted a spell. She hurtled forward with a pop and narrowly missed a tree before she spun her body and landed on her feet, her wand still at the ready.

The red lights stopped as Raine, Cameron, and Asher approached from different angles. They weren't a single diffuse source of illumination but two long, narrow crimson beams that cut through the darkness like head-lights from a tiny car.

"I don't think that's from a student," Raine murmured and raised her wand.

The bushes shook, and a small form stepped out. The

soft incandescence of the light orbs revealed a small rabbit —or at least what appeared to be a small rabbit, albeit not the normal kind. The creature's fur was dark red and its eyes were the source of the two red beams.

"That's definitely not a student," she said and lowered her wand. It was hard to be intimidated by a rabbit, even if it did have glowing beams for eyes.

"Nope." Asher grinned and moved aside to create an opening for the animal to escape. "I think it might be some kind of pooka relative."

The creature sprinted past the Wood Elf into the darkened forest and its lights receded.

"From what I've read about pooka, they are a little more mischievous and can change shapes," Raine said. "Even if the beam eyes are similar."

Cameron stared in the direction of the dwindling red lights. "It could be a pooka, a pooka relative, or something else entirely. That's why we're here—to figure out everything that's on this island."

Josephine seemed pleased. "It's always wonderful to find something new."

"We should get back." Raine gestured in the direction of the camp, at least as far she could remember. If Asher and Josephine didn't know the way back, Cameron could follow the scent trail. "I think we're close to the time limit."

She spared one last glance in the direction of the retreating red rabbit. When they had arrived, the normal-looking trees made her doubt how exotic the research trip would be, but the last few hours had changed everything. Beam-eyed rabbits, glowing plants, and other wonders awaited. Maybe the outer layer of trees served as camou-flage for the more fantastic interior.

Asher yawned and moved past her. "It was fun getting to know you." He glanced at Cameron, who frowned. "And I look forward to getting to know you better, Raine."

CHAPTER SIX

Unaccountably restless, Raine turned on her side in bed. Complete darkness smothered the cabin, along with a stillness she rarely experienced in her room at the School of Necessary Magic, even when her roommates weren't there. There was always some small distant noise to remind her that she was surrounded by people at the school, unlike New Firefly Island and the current tiny population.

"Are you still awake, Raine?" Sara asked. "It sounds like you're moving."

"You know what my moving in bed sounds like?" She laughed.

Her friend sat up. A small, dim light orb appeared in her palm and highlighted her face. "I've been your roommate for a while. So, yes, I know."

Evie sat up and stretched. "What's going on?" she murmured, sleepiness slurring her words.

"Nothing," Raine said with a sigh. "I didn't mean to wake anyone up, especially with how late it already is."

"It's no big deal." The kitsune raised her arm and the orb drifted upward until it floated near the roof of the windowless cabin. "They said they would let us rest tomorrow anyway. It doesn't matter if we stay up late. We might be on a research trip, but this is also the summer. We're spending it together, so we should make some summer memories."

Raine brushed a few rogue strands of hair out of her eyes. "What do you think of the Orono students?"

"They are definitely interesting." Sara lay back and tucked her hands beneath her head. "And different, too. I don't know. It's weird. It's not like I never meet other magicals who aren't from our school, but interacting with a group of magical students from another school is strange."

"I know what you mean. We've spent three years at the School of Necessary Magic. In my case, I had very little contact with magicals before I found out about my powers, so to me, the school, students, and professors are what magic is."

Evie mumbled something, but her eyes were already closed. Raine smiled softly over at her sleepy friend.

"Kelly seems cool," the kitsune said, her brow puckered. "But she's really competitive. That wasn't a problem since I can be competitive too, but she was obsessed with winning the game."

Raine snorted quietly. "I think Asher was less interested in the game than me."

Her friend's eyes widened. "What do you mean?"

"He...um, expressed interest. Romantic or whatever you want to call it." She smiled a little shyly. "I wouldn't put it past him to have suggested the pairings so he could end up with me. From what he told me, their group are all friends but none of them are dating."

"Kelly would have to relax for five seconds to date someone from what I saw tonight." Sara grinned. "Does Cameron know?"

"I didn't tell him directly, but I did make it clear to Asher that I wasn't interested. I also let him know we're all with someone so he wouldn't bother anyone else."

The other girl snickered. "Is he that desperate?"

"I don't know if I'd say he's desperate. He took it well. Our school's a lot bigger than his, so there are more options for him, I guess. I—" Her breath caught as a powerful pulse of magic surged and seemed to travel past her. "Did you feel that?"

Sara frowned and nodded. "Yes, I did. I wonder what it was."

The ground shook and the cabin with it. Raine gritted her teeth at the odd sensation and her stomach churned in response to the shuddering movement. A book on the history of organized crime she had brought fell from the wooden chest at the foot of her bed. Her robe hung on a rack along the wall fell next. A fallen book and robe didn't represent mass destruction, but that didn't help her stomach to settle.

Evie's eyes flickered open, and she sat up with a yelp. "What's going on?"

"Another earthquake," the kitsune told her.

Raine scrambled down her bed toward the chest. She needed her wand. All the magic in the world was useless if you couldn't cast a spell.

The tremor stopped.

She took a few quick breaths before she snatched the robe and her wand from the chest and headed toward the door. Evie and Sara hopped out of bed, although the witch left her wand on her chest and the kitsune didn't take any of her pouches.

The three girls emerged from the cabin to find the Orono girls already outside, a few light orbs above them and deep scowls on their faces. The boys from both schools emerged next, and the professors joined them seconds later.

Professor Tarelli arrived last and a frosty mist wafted out of her open cabin. Ice coated the inside of the door.

"Is anyone hurt?" Professor Powell surveyed the students with a look of deep concern.

They shook their heads, although everyone seemed a little shaken.

"Did you feel it?" Raine asked.

Professor Tarelli nodded. "It was hard not to feel the earthquake, Evie."

Raine sighed, more disappointed than annoyed. How long would it take for the Nyran to remember who she was? "I'm Raine, and no, not the quake, the magic right before it. There was definitely a pulse of magic."

The professor frowned. "I was asleep." She looked at the other three professors, who shrugged.

Sara gestured toward their nearby cabin. "I felt a big pulse of magic too."

"As did I." Josephine nodded firmly as if to emphasize her agreement.

Finn grunted. The Louper player looked annoyed. "Some big magic, yeah. I was about to fall asleep, too."

Professor Kaylis cleared his throat and stepped forward. "That only adds more support to the theory that the underlying cause of the tremors is magical in nature. We've not sensed that kind of magic before, but we might not if the actual magical source emitted in the wrong direction or is oscillating or something of that nature. We should take note of it for future geological teams, but it's beyond the scope of our particular expedition to identify the exact cause. That said, if we happen to stumble upon the cause, it's not like we can't claim credit for it."

"And you're not worried?" Professor Powell asked, a skeptical look on his face.

"Why would I be worried? This island is known for these minor tremors, and the earthquake wasn't any more severe than the ones we've already experienced over the last few days. This is merely the first one that happened in the middle of the night since our arrival. That's another possible explanation for feeling the magic."

Professor Hudson stared at her cabin, her eyes narrowed. "We should check for cracks. There could be structural damage."

"Of course, of course." Professor Kaylis yawned. "Safety first, but I'm not too concerned as none of the previous quakes did any damage. But, of course, it wouldn't hurt to check, and it would be an excellent exercise. Always be prepared. I trust your students are capable of simple spell repairs—all but Cameron, obviously."

The shifter frowned and folded his arms over his chest. Raine gave him a reassuring smile.

"Yes," Professor Hudson said. "Of course."

The Orono professor clapped approvingly. "Excellent! I doubt we would need something like that, however. Check for cracks and that sort of thing and take all the time you need. We won't force anyone up at dawn tomorrow or any such nonsense."

Evie waved to catch their attention. "I packed a few repair potions if we need them. I didn't know what we might use, so I brought a few different ones." She gasped. "I should check on them and make sure they didn't break." She scurried toward their door.

Raine raised her wand and summoned her own light orb. She might not be able to prepare for magical earthquakes, but she could fix a few cracks in a wooden cabin.

CHAPTER SEVEN

Raine swallowed another bite of eggs. The shells might have been a strange mottled color, and she'd never heard of the type of Oriceran bird that had laid them, but they tasted like normal chicken eggs to her. Maybe the actual birds tasted like chicken too.

The students from both schools sat around the tables. The professors were all gathered in Professor Kaylis' cabin to plan groups and assignments for the next few days. Other than providing the ingredients for the late brunch, they'd kept out of the young people's way.

Both groups of students had exchanged stories about their schools. Raine had briefly highlighted their misadventures with Hap in the kemana and the trouble with the druids soon after her arrival. The Orono students had shared a few funny anecdotes and Finn was now in the middle of their latest tale.

He grinned. "So, there we were. No one wanted to admit to the professors that we screwed up when we messed around with Good Ol' Basil's transformation potion after he specifically told us only to do it with him around. We had our boy Harris running around campus as a giant hamster. Yeah, he was only a few feet long, but that's still big for a hamster, and I swear the potion made his teeth extra sharp." He grimaced and shook his hand out as if the memory was all too vivid. "How uncool would it be to lose a hand to a hamster?"

Josephine sighed, her hand to her face. "You should have gone to the professors from the start. I told you that at the time. It would have saved us all a lot of trouble."

"You're usually right, Jo, but hey, you sometimes want to avoid the inevitable for as long as possible." Finn shrugged and high-fived Asher.

Adrien frowned. "I don't understand. Why was he running around? Why didn't he want to be returned to his normal form?"

"That's the thing." Finn shook his head. "The professor didn't explain at the time that the potion didn't preserve your normal mind when you changed forms, so Harris wasn't only a wizard in giant hamster form. He was a giant hamster with giant hamster instincts. And a fast little guy, too, in addition to those nasty teeth." He smirked with dark humor. "But our boy Asher, here, convinced us all we could get out of the situation without too much trouble."

The elf laughed and slapped his knee. "We had to take turns to go around and create distractions so the professors wouldn't catch on. We didn't know how to undo the magic at first, and we hoped it would run out."

Raine smiled. Although the Orono students didn't seem to be a true trouble squad, they obviously were still close friends who had their share of adventures together.

The corners of Cameron's mouth turned up in a wicked grin. "It didn't wear off, though, did it?"

Finn and Asher looked at each other and burst out laughing.

Kelly snorted and rolled her eyes. "It wasn't that funny at the time." She muttered something foul under her breath. "They used the stupid potion in the morning, and it was close on dinner by then, and Harris was still a hamster. Rumors were all over campus about the 'Doom Hamster.'"

Raine's brow lifted. "Doom Hamster?"

The witch shrugged. "I don't know how that even started. No one ever admitted to it, but by dinner, the professors were out in force, half-convinced that some crazed Oriceran monster had been summoned to the school and could breathe fire. I was sure they would tell us to gather in the cafeteria and prepare to be attacked." She flicked her hand accusingly toward Asher. "All the while, he continued to assure us, 'We have it under control. Don't worry.'"

The elf winked. "We did have it under control. Silas and Heidi's quick research at least revealed the kind of magic we needed to reverse the transformation. We only needed more time."

Kelly scoffed. "We didn't have any experience with the magic. Your master plan to hide Harris until we knew what to do was lame, Asher."

"I admit, there were a few details that needed to be worked out, but we did have things under control until the Doom Hamster charged the headmaster. I've never seen the old man whip off a spell so quickly. I was scared he would blast Harris with a fireball, but instead, chains appeared." Asher pantomimed a flick of a wand. "All the professors rushed out there like Rhazdon had attacked the school with a squadron of dragons and a fleet of Kraken ready to emerge from the river."

He cackled with real mirth. "It was the funniest thing ever. All these high-powered magicals scared of a giant hamster. That was when Kaylis wandered out, looking confused, and without missing a beat, he said, 'Oh, wait. *That's* the hamster everyone's talking about?'" The elf howled with laughter and slapped his thigh before he wiped his eyes. "He said, 'It's a great time to test another potion,' and poured the concoction over Harris before the headmaster even knew what was going on."

Kelly shook her head, her cheeks slightly red.

Raine stared at Asher. "And you didn't get in trouble?"

"Oh, no, we got in major trouble, me most of all. We couldn't leave school grounds for a while after that, and we had all kinds of extra chores." Asher rubbed his hands together. "But it was worth it to see the look on the headmaster's face."

Adrien stared at the Orono elf and curiosity battled confusion on his face. "This might sound rude, but does that sort of thing happen to you often?"

"Oh, not that exact thing, but we do have a lot of fun at our school." He sighed happily. "It's good to be in a magical academy, right?"

"How can I put this delicately..."

Raine's jaw tightened. The other Trouble Squad members exchanged looks as all tried to decide who should be the one to stop their friend from offending the Orono students.

Asher waved a hand dismissively. "Honestly is the best policy, I always say. Lay it on me, Adrien."

"We've had various adventures and misadventures at the School of Necessary Magic," the Light Elf said when the confusion on his face finally defeated curiosity. "Many were dangerous, like what happened with the druids. Although it's not bizarre that strange things might happen at a magic school, we have, for the most part, not gone out of our way to look for trouble. It has always sort of found us."

"Although Raine can't let anything go," Cameron said with a smile.

Sara grinned and nodded. "I fear for all the criminals she confronts in the future. Not only that, if someone needs help, I think she'd die rather than not help them."

The Orono students all looked at Raine and her cheeks heated under the unexpected attention.

"The point is," Adrien continued, "that in most of our cases, it was either a person in trouble or someone who attacked us for whatever reason." His expression darkened. "We've developed a relationship with the professors wherein they trust us and know we won't go off and do strange things simply because we can. I presume that relationship is at the core of why they selected us for the trip."

Asher leaned forward. "And you wonder why a group of real troublemakers was selected?"

Raine sighed. "He doesn't mean anything by it. He's merely...straightforward."

Josephine cleared her throat quietly. "If I were in Adrien's place, I would wonder the same thing." She looked at her friend and raised an eyebrow.

The Wood Elf's smile faltered for a second. "That part of Maine has a lot of weirdness, especially magical creatures. It turns out that as good as we are at causing trouble, we're also good at ending it. We've helped stop more than a few actually dangerous critters, including one time where these magic-seeking hungry worm things were somehow released in Orono. And we've had a few wacky things happen in the Bar Harbor kemana too." He leaned forward to whisper his next words. "But we're not supposed to talk about them like I bet you have a few things you're not supposed to talk about." He straightened and spoke at a normal volume. "We don't have a cool nickname like you guys, but we're the unofficial magical beast control around our school. Even the professors admit that we have great instincts."

Kelly ran her tongue over her bottom lip. "I think that's why Old Basil wanted us. For whatever reason, we handle magical creatures well, so we're the perfect ones to deal with any that get out of hand—except when we're the reason for them." She grinned. "And you're the FBI Trouble Squad, so you can handle all kinds of trouble." She peered intently at Raine. "We heard that the School of Necessary Magic had something to do with identifying that there was a dangerous bug in Arc Eighty-Eight. It wasn't huge at our school, but Silas was into it in a big way."

The shy wizard shrugged and his face reddened.

Raine's heart rate immediately lurched up a notch. Of all their adventures, the legacy of Arc Eighty-Eight might last the longest.

"You could say that." She sighed. "I don't want to go into all the details, but basically, a character from the game came alive at our school. She ended up being powerful enough to draw us into her world, and we were almost trapped there."

"Woah. Seriously? That's crazy." Kelly looked horrified

Raine nodded. "We defeated her, but after that, she came into the real world. Somehow, she separated her soul into two parts—two Coral Elf sisters, one shy and one angry. They ended up attending classes while they tried to figure out a way to stabilize themselves."

Asher stared at her. "You're messing with us, right? This is weird even by magical standards."

"If only," Cameron muttered.

Adrien nodded his agreement, his shoulders more relaxed than before. With his curiosity sated, much of the tension had fled his face.

She nodded. "No one knew at first, of course, but when we were dragged into the mess with Eris, the sisters were there as well. It turns out that they didn't have enough power to continue living for much longer, and they were looking for something to help them with that." She sighed. "In the end, they found what they needed, but it was only enough for one of them—the shy one, Madelyn."

Asher demonstrated something he hadn't in all their encounters before—silence and shock.

Josephine shook her head. "Let's set aside the fact that you casually mentioned that you personally faced off against the Witch Queen of Chaos. You're saying a whole new life was created by the game at your school, and now...what, is this Madelyn a student of the School of Necessary Magic?"

Raine shrugged. "For now. From what we were told, the

PDA doesn't know what to do with her, and Headmistress Berens has taken responsibility until they work it out."

The Orono students stared at Raine in silence. Asher sat with his jaw agape and Josephine blinked as she processed the information. Everyone turned toward Finn when he started clapping.

"Your school is crazy," he said and sounded genuinely impressed. "Straight-up crazy, but it also sounds awesome, and you guys are awesome. We've had some weird adventures, but nothing approaching that. You showed us up, Raine." He bowed in exaggerated deference, a grin on his face.

She sighed and shook her head. "That wasn't what I tried to do."

Asher managed to shut his mouth and smiled before he spoke. "I heard what they said earlier. You like to help people. Sometimes, with magicals, things will be complicated. I think it's cool. We all do. We couldn't ask for a better group to help us out during this project."

The Orono students all grinned in agreement.

Asher nodded and his eyes twinkled. "Now, let me tell you about this teleporting acid-spitting butterfly we had to catch in our sophomore year."

CHAPTER EIGHT

D ays later, Professor Powell stood in a swaying rowboat and surveyed the teams while he tapped his wand against his palm. The fifteen students had been separated into five groups of three and assigned their own rowboats. The small fleet of young magicals floated near the dock and the students clutched wands, except for Cameron who held an oar tightly with both hands.

"Let me be clear since this is the first time I've dealt with all of you on my own," the professor shouted. "I have full authority over both groups. After discussion with Professor Kaylis, we agreed I'd be best suited to help you practice the necessary locomotion spells."

He pointed his wand toward the rocky beach. "We've spent these last few days doing little jaunts into the forest, and everyone should now understand that even with our magic, there are limits to our travel ability. We're not about to cut down the forest to make a road, so that brings us back to something Professor Kaylis told me even before I arrived." He pointed to his boat. "He told me that we'll need to take advantage of these boats to move around quickly."

Cameron groaned quietly from the craft he shared with Raine and Kelly, but the professor had cast the anti-seasickness spell on him, so at least he didn't look completely miserable.

Finn raised his hand. "Hey, Professor Powell."

Xander nodded to the boy. "Yes?"

"Why not simply teach us a water-walking spell or something? Why bother with boats?" He tugged on his life-jacket as if to highlight his displeasure.

"If you lose your wand in an accident, that boat might very well save your life." Professor Powell made several quick movements with his wand and rattled off a complicated incantation. After that, he stepped onto the water and didn't sink, but the choppy waves still splashed water on his pants and boots.

"For one thing, this spell demands a significant amount of energy." He gestured to his pants before he stepped back into his rowboat. "That's another reason. The other is that it's hard to carry as much gear. We don't want to risk the quick-transfer scrolls you've used for notes either."

He tapped his wand against the side of his head. "Always remember, the best way to use magic is often to enhance something you already have rather than replace it completely." He knelt. "You don't have to use as much magic, and it will generally be easier and quicker. That has utility, and it might save your life, too, when you think about it that way."

Asher's face quirked into a smirk but he didn't say anything.

Professor Powell pointed his wand toward the back of his boat. "The good thing about everything I'm about to teach you is that it's really applied versions of magic you already know with some slight modifications, rather than something completely new. Basically, we'll combine shield spells with similar magic to burst spells. You reduce the drag on the boat and you propel it with the other spell. It's more challenging to do and maintain both spells on your own, but you all have at least two active casters on each boat. For now, let me demonstrate what I'm talking about first."

A few precise movements of his wand accompanied his incantations, and a faint shimmer surrounded the boat.

"It's better if you can see the shield." Professor Powell shook his wand a few times. "It's a nice visual reminder that you have the prerequisites to get the boat moving as efficiently as possible with the next step." He pointed his wand and spoke the next incantation slowly. The bulk of it sounded similar to a burst spell, but the ending was different.

His craft surged forward.

Raine gasped. She'd expected the rowboat to glide through the water, not cut through the waves like a rocket.

A grin on his face, the professor shifted his wand and the boat turned with it to narrowly avoid another one containing Evie, William, and Adrien. Some water splashed them, however, and fire appeared in the half-Ifrit's eyes.

The fast-moving craft slowed. Professor Powell repeated his incantation and it increased speed again. "You won't have to constantly recast the spell. I'm merely feeding it minimal direct magic as a demonstration. You'll practice over the next couple of days and get a feel for the right amount of magic you need to channel into a boat for the speed you need." He twisted his wand, and his small vessel jerked almost ninety degrees to its side. The sudden change killed its momentum and water splashed inside. "You'll also have practice with water movement spells. Since you'll be in groups, a good strategy is to have someone driving at all times, someone maintaining the shield, and someone bailing water if necessary. When you get good enough at this sort of thing, you can actually move in a wooden boat like it's a speedboat. I once traveled the entire Amazon this way."

He gazed off into the distance and smiled. "That was indeed an...interesting summer. I was almost eaten three times." He shook his head and returned his attention to the lesson. "Anyway, it's time to get started. Let's do this one by one. Raine, Kelly, and Cameron, we'll start with you. Obviously, Cameron can't contribute to the spells, but he needs to adjust to being in boats, which is why I didn't excuse him from this lesson."

The shifter muttered under his breath.

Kelly lifted her wand. "I'll handle the shield first if you want to try to move us."

Raine nodded and waited for the other witch to cast the shield spell over the boat before she drew a deep breath and pointed her wand toward the back. The incantation followed, each syllable spoken slowly and deliberately as she made the necessary motions and fed a small amount of magic in. Their boat jerked forward, not nearly as fast as the professor's had but not at a crawl either.

With her heart pounding, she turned slowly and twisted

her wand—clutched tightly with both hands—and the craft bounced a few times over the waves. Her stomach lurched, but she ignored the sensation and concentrated on steering.

Cameron clutched his oar even tighter, his knuckles almost white and a stern look on his face. "This isn't as bad as I thought, but I can't imagine what it would feel like if I didn't have that spell on me."

The boat slowed until it finally stopped and bobbed up and down on the incoming waves.

Professor Powell smiled. "Excellent, Raine. A good initial showing. Good technique."

She exhaled a sigh of relief. While she occasionally fell into the negative habit of believing she might never have the natural talent or power of some of the other witches at her school, she was learning to recognize this particular weakness. Years of careful attention to detail in all aspects of her life had helped to steadily improve her magical skill.

The professor pointed to the rowboat with Dnai, Sara, and Philip. "You're up next. I want everyone to have a try at manning one of the stations. We'll switch places to make that possible, and depending on your progress, maybe I'll let you putter along the beach without direct supervision."

Dnai sniffed disdainfully. "Professor, I want to point out that I can fly." She shrugged and extended her wings a few inches.

"Sure, but you're still participating in this exercise. It's easier to carry people and things in a boat than when you fly. So, let's see it. Decide amongst yourselves who will do what."

After a brief discussion, Sara chose to maintain the

shields while Philip worked on the propulsion. Dnai wanted to focus on water control.

The wizard raised his wand and took a deep a few deep breaths before he shouted the spell rapidly. Raine winced when she recognized a few wrong syllables in the middle and some incorrect pitch emphasis.

The boat hurtled forward and up and continued headlong in actual flight. The two girls yelped, and Philip groaned.

A few seconds later, it splashed into the water upside down. The three students emerged from beneath it and spat water out while the others laughed.

Professor Powell offered an apologetic smile to the three soaked students. "I think a couple of observations and reminders are called for. Slow and steady is fine until you master the incantation, and it's better to start out with too little power than too much." He raised his wand and waved it. The capsized boat righted itself as if it were the simplest thing in the world. "Also, a reminder that wet wands still work with no problems."

Dnai crawled into the boat with a pained expression. "My poor wings. I'll smell like salt forever." She sighed and pushed wet clumps of her dark hair to either side of her face.

Philip shoved Sara into the boat before he scrambled in himself. "Sorry." His efforts made it rock and he clutched the gunwale with slight panic on his face. "What's in the water around here?"

The professor shrugged. "I doubt that there's anything worse than a few sharks or maybe a few giant bugs.

Nothing serious. It's probably more that the magic has scared off larger sea creatures than anything dangerous."

The young wizard frowned. "Seriously, du...uh... Professor, sharks and giant bugs? Those are okay?" He shook the water off his wand. "Wait. What counts as a giant bug?"

"The sharks are all small. Don't think Great White, let alone megalodon. They're more scared of you than you are of them."

"Maybe," Philip muttered but didn't seem at all reassured.

Professor Powell scratched his chin. "As for the other issue, does a bug the size of a small dog count? Or is that merely large?"

Philip's eyes widened. "That's not a real thing, is it?" He looked around in desperation.

"Keep practicing and don't fall out, and you won't have to worry."

CHAPTER NINE

Professor Kaylis offered the students sitting around the firepit a broad smile. A small cauldron sat atop a metal grate.

"Ah. I almost forget. I've already told this to the Orono students, but for our friends from the School of Necessary Magic, it's perhaps best that I repeat myself. For travel reasons, we didn't have you pack a cauldron, nor did we bring many, but it's no worry." He swiped his arm in a bold gesture to point at the boiling black cauldron. "I'll handle the potions prep for your first freshwater potion, and people can use my cauldron as necessary throughout the trip if you want to make more. It might not be necessary at all."

Philip, who sat close to him at a table with Sara and Dnai, nodded quickly. He did a poor job of hiding his boredom.

Evie sat hunched over her notepad, a pen in hand and her face alight with interest. Raine sat beside her and admitted, at least to herself, that she didn't find the subject of today's lecture as engaging as some of the others. Still, she managed not to allow open boredom to show on her face like Philip.

Sara shrugged. "Why not simply make water directly? This seems like unnecessary work."

Professor Kaylis shook a finger at her. "That's a good question, Sara. You could, but it means you need to stop, cast the spell, and potentially tax your magical resources that you might have drawn on all day." The wizard fumbled in one of the many pockets in his shorts and withdrew a small vial. "Of course, you've brought fresh water on your initial forays into the forest, but what if you drink it all? In the case of the witches and wizards, they might lose their wands and find they have trouble managing even a quick spell."

He clucked his tongue and regarded them with a sober expression. "At which point, a few drops of this freshwater potion would come in very handy, as it can change a good gallon or so of salt water into fresh water, no new magic required." He shook the potion. "That's something you students always forget. If you can prepare something ahead of time in potion form, it's always preferable to an active spell." He tucked the container into his pocket. "Even if it isn't as flashy."

Evie and Raine scribbled notes as they always did. Among the others, Silas and Heidi paid close attention, but the remaining students—both from Charlottesville and Orono—seemed less interested. Philip's eyes fluttered constantly as if he might doze off.

The professor raised a small aquamarine petal from the table in his forefingers. "I already showed you the primary ingredients, all of which are fairly easy to obtain, and many of you have already seen the flowers this petal comes from. They are not unique to this island, but they are rare on Earth outside areas of high magic concentration such as here or the kemanas."

He looked aside for a moment and a thoughtful expression settled on his face. "I should note that they aren't the only thing that will work. Traitor's Weed is something common that would also serve well enough as the primary ingredient. Frost Kiss is another excellent choice. Swirling Violet is decent, although it won't do as well. It would maybe convert half a gallon." He took a mortar and pestle from a nearby table and began to grind the petals. "The truth is, the potion itself is fairly simple. Add the ingredients, boil for about an hour, and you're good to go. It's merely a potion that the average magical won't need, so students rarely learn it."

Asher grinned. "Yeah. Why bother with a potion when you can go to a water fountain or sink?"

Several of the students chuckled.

Professor Kaylis smiled with no hint of offense on his face. "True enough, but as I hope this trip is reinforcing, there are different types of dependencies, whether technological or magical, and it's important to be able to account for those." He frowned at his cauldron and gestured for the students to move away. "Did someone use this cauldron earlier? Or yesterday?"

The students stood hurriedly and took several steps back. Raine's heart kicked into a gallop.

Philip's eyes widened, and he grabbed Sara and practically carried her several yards back. She rolled her eyes at her boyfriend.

Silas raised his hand timidly. "I used it yesterday. I asked Professor Tarelli, and she said it was okay. It was for only about thirty minutes. You were still out with a survey group."

The professor scratched his cheek. "I see, and of course she said it was okay. That much was fine." He backed away slowly as his cauldron began to bubble with angry fury. "She merely forgot to mention it to me. Silas, my boy, do me a favor next time and let me know directly. We all know that Professor Tarelli can be a touch absent-minded, and that can lead to issues."

The student blinked and looked decidedly nervous. "Is something wrong?"

Raine raised her wand and cast a shield spell and the other students hastily followed suit. Philip moved in front of Sara. William tried to do the same for Evie, but she evaded him, her gaze fixed on the bubbling potion.

Cameron had been excused from the lecture due to his shifter nature and lack of general potion-making ability. He had told Raine he would take a run in wolf form.

Professor Kaylis frowned as he squinted at his potion. "Let me guess, Silas. You were strengthening an already prepared flare potion yesterday?"

The boy nodded quickly. "Yes. I brought a few but they are old, so I thought I'd freshen them using that technique you showed us last semester. They were supposed to be back-up in case we ran into something nasty in the woods. How did you know?"

"Some of the ingredients you used can cross-react with

the ingredients in this potion—even at very low concentrations—in surprisingly violent ways." The man laughed and his jolly smile lingered. "Let this be a lesson to all of you. The scouring spells and potions I recommend—and I'm sure the potions teacher at the other school also recommends—aren't merely a suggestion. Magical contamination is the bane of any potions maker. You can clean a cauldron thoroughly and go weeks without trouble, or not clean a cauldron effectively and find yourself in trouble hours later."

Raine frowned. She had never thought much about cauldron clean-up. They were required to attend to their cauldrons in class, but the scouring potions were always provided. Professor Fowler had idly mentioned that they would learn how to brew the potions in their senior year due to their complexity and specificity of use.

Students without experienced potion makers around them weren't supposed to make potions outside of school anyway. In practical terms, that meant Evie was one of the few of the FBI Trouble Squad who did much with this type of magic on vacation.

The frothing liquid in the cauldron bubbled and hissed and a few sparks erupted from the surface.

Professor Kaylis raised his wand and his grin built so much that it looked like it must hurt. "Don't worry. Sometimes, failure provides the most entertaining mistakes of all." He chanted a quick spell and a column of radiance surrounded the firepit and cauldron and extended into the sky. A thin plane of light extended beneath the grate. "It doesn't hurt to take a few precautions, though. There's no reason to waste a perfectly good healing potion."

The cauldron began to shake and rattle on the grate. Raine layered another shield spell over herself to be safe. With a loud explosion, it shattered into tiny pieces. The frothing liquid inside splattered against the walls and floor of the magical shield around it. The shards of the vessel settled in an uneven pile, still hissing and sparking.

The professor laughed with genuine amusement. "Now that's what I call a good cauldron death."

Raine blinked several times at the destruction. Potion accidents at the School of Necessary Magic didn't normally destroy the cauldron, but it might have been that the wizard welcomed the damage as an object lesson.

Silas winced. "Sorry, Professor."

Professors Hudson and Tarelli rushed out of their cabins. The concern vanished from both their faces once they spotted their colleague standing in front of the column of light with a huge grin on his face.

Professor Tarelli rolled her eyes. "Did you do it on purpose this time, Basil?"

He grinned with no offense at all. "No. A simple accident."

Professor Hudson sighed and shook her head.

The wizard turned his attention to Silas. "It's nothing, my boy. A mere inconvenience. Because I'm an always-prepared potions master, this really is a trivial problem to correct." He scrabbled in his pocket for another vial and shook it after a quick glance as if to confirm that it was the right one. "Can anyone guess what this is?"

"A repair potion?" Evie asked.

"Indeed. Good job. A particular type that I keep around specifically for cauldron repairs."

William had managed to creep in front of Evie. Fire glowed in his eyes, but Professor Kaylis seemed oblivious to the boy's concern.

Raine eyed the professor dubiously. "Your cauldron blows up so much that you always have special potions on hand to fix it?"

Professor Kaylis marched over to the glowing column. "Exploring the edge of potion making always involves some risk, which typically manifests as an exploding cauldron." He pressed his hand with the vial against the column and after a few seconds, it penetrated but moved slowly as if pushing through a thick gel. He upended the receptacle and poured the potion over the remnants of the cauldron.

A bright flash blinded Raine. When her vision cleared, the vessel was half-reassembled. Small chunks flew back into place and cracks sealed themselves.

Philip shook his head. "No offense, Professor, but I think I'll leave the potion making to you for a while."

CHAPTER TEN

Professor Hudson's careful control of a rowboat relieved the students of any risk of capsizing. It'd only been a few days since their first lessons. Laden with Raine, Asher, Adrien, and Finn, the professor's craft cruised along the eastern coast of the island.

Adrien helped with water bailing, but Professor Hudson handled both the shielding and propulsion without help.

Raine felt her backpack to make sure it was closed and her quick-transfer scroll was protected from any water. The scrolls allowed them to take voice notes and copy them to a central book Professor Tarelli had set up in her cabin, a necessity given their inability to use electronic or radio data transfer.

Their camp lay in the southwest corner of the island. The entire western side was far more accessible, with longer stretches of beaches. Even if they were irregular and rock-strewn, they were at least visible, unlike some of the barely submerged rocky shoals that dominated the eastern portion of the island. The beaches might never become tourist attractions, but they made docking easier.

The eastern side, in contrast, was defined more by jagged rocks that required caution. While twenty-first-century magicals weren't at tremendous risk, they still needed to be alert.

"We're almost there," Professor Hudson announced. "The section we'll explore in the northeast hasn't been studied by any of our teams yet, so we don't know what to expect. Obviously, we don't believe it will be more dangerous than any of the other areas we explored. Caution is never unwarranted, though."

"Woah." Finn pointed into the distance. "What's that?"

Raine squinted but couldn't see anything other than water. A few seconds later, two dark fins broke through the surface.

"I see it!" Asher yelled. "Is that what I think it is?"

"Yeah, I think it is. Cool." A grin broke out on Finn's face.

Adrien narrowed his eyes. "Should we be worried? Novelty might be interesting, but it can still present danger."

Professor Hudson glanced toward the fins, her wand still pointed at the back of the boat. "If that's what I think it is, no. Let's take a moment to watch and verify." She slowed the craft.

The parallel dark fins glided through the water. Whatever creature they belonged to didn't appear to swim directly toward the boat, but its course would intercept the island in a few minutes if it held the same speed.

"Keep watching," Professor Hudson said and raised her

wand. The rowboat slowed to almost a stop and only the weak tide tugged it gradually toward the nearby shore.

A huge, dark form leapt out of the water. The two upper fins were mirrored by two dark ones on the bottom and another two pairs on either side of its smooth, shiny body. Easily twenty-feet long, the bulbous creature had four solid green eyes spaced equally around the sides of its head and which glinted in the afternoon sun. A thin line, a mouth perhaps, cut through the center, but it didn't open before it splashed into the water. It wasn't until the creature dove that Raine noticed it had two wriggling tails.

She smiled. "It's not a whale, but it's close."

Asher nodded. "Those go by a lot of names, but Professor Tarelli's called them skimmers. We saw one on our way to the island when we took the ferry."

"Not fair. I didn't see anything on my trip."

"What can I say? We're lucky in Orono." The elf winked.

The skimmer submerged until only its top fins remained visible. It changed direction, this time heading farther out into the ocean and away from the island.

Professor Hudson pointed with her free hand at the retreating fins. "As strange as it looks compared to surface Earth life, it's a filter-feeder from my understanding, with only a small amount of magic required to sustain it. As the gates continue to open, you'll see many new types of life continue to flourish."

The fins submerged as the skimmer vanished below the surface.

"Aren't there concerns about invasive species?" Raine asked.

"Indeed, the careful balance of existing species and

reintroduced Oriceran species is a subject of continued concern and research." Professor Hudson cast a new propulsion spell, and the boat kicked forward. "Which is why endeavors such as the Magical Multitudes Project are so important. In some cases, we might have new species coming over or transported over from Oriceran. In others, the increasing level of magic leads to them re-colonizing areas or expanding their range away from preserves like this. The more we learn about what is out there and what might be coming, the better we can help to smooth the transition."

Asher laughed. "Aren't the gates supposed to take thousands of years to open? It's not like we have to worry that much. A few skimmers here and there isn't the same thing as dragons over every city." He glanced at Raine. "I wish we had a dragon at our school like you do."

She shrugged apologetically. They really were lucky to have a resident dragon.

Professor Hudson gave him a thin smile and shook her head. "The little magic that has initially returned has already fundamentally changed Earth. Even if a potential problem lay far in the future, careful work by each generation can help ameliorate the negative effects. As magicals, we also tend to live longer and can put more effort into such things. It's something to think about. Part of our reasoning behind this trip is to help you understand such things."

"Not everything that's magical, even if it is an animal, is peaceful," Adrien said with a frown. "There are some really nasty creatures on Oriceran—predators the average non-magical couldn't even begin to handle. We won't be able to leave everything alone."

Finn and Asher both nodded their agreement with unusually serious looks on their faces.

"Of course." Professor Hudson nodded toward the trees that covered the side of the island. "No one claims otherwise. This is a research project, so we're trying to exercise restraint, but it's not as if anyone suggests that deadly creatures will be allowed to roam unchecked. There is a difference between deadly and merely inconvenient, and that's something that's often forgotten, even when it comes to non-magical creatures."

Raine shook her head. "One thing I've learned from studying all my FBI materials is that our laws are way behind on everything magical. The fact that I'll be the first publicly acknowledged witch in the FBI is proof of that." She sighed. "Our laws are based on so many assumptions about what and who a person is and what they might be capable of. I'm always surprised by how many bad presuppositions there are and how they don't seem to want to accept the reality of magic."

"All things change with time." A thoughtful expression settled over the professor's face. "I always think I am lucky to be born in a time of such transition. There are so many opportunities to observe how societies change fundamentally. We'll now have a strong understanding of such issues that many of our ancestors could have used."

Adrien frowned as if he couldn't quite believe her. "You feel lucky? Even with all the danger and chaos? They didn't need magical bounty hunters before the gates opened. It used to be that the Griffins and a few others could handle most trouble, and now..." He scoffed and shook his head.

"What you're saying is true, Adrien, but incomplete," Professor Hudson responded.

"Incomplete?"

"Yes. It's never been the case, even without magic, that either world was completely at peace. All we can do is be part of the solution, and one way to do that is to make sure we're equipped with the most relevant knowledge possible."

A humanoid shadow passed between two trees.

Raine's breath caught. "Are we the only ones on this side of the island today?"

The professor nodded. "Yes. There's a team that will survey an area in the north, but they're traveling up the west side of the island. That group includes Professor Kaylis, William, Evie, Dnai, and Silas, I believe."

"I could have sworn I saw someone walking in the forest over there." She frowned and pointed at the trees.

Asher and Finn exchanged glances before they turned to her and said simultaneously, "Mirror cats."

"Mirror cats?"

The elf nodded. "Professor Tarelli mentioned them. They are jaguar-sized and can generate illusions when they hunt, but the illusions are based on things around them. Uh...you could say they mirror things. It's not like Wood Elf camouflage, but it's not as good as the invisibility from a stealth spell either."

"If it's mirror cats and they have reflected fake people, wouldn't that mean there's someone near them?"

He shook his head. "Not if they've mirrored us. We're

probably some weird monster from their perspective given that we're heading through the waterway faster than anything else they might see."

"Okay. I guess that makes sense." She blinked. "Wait. There are illusion-generating jaguars on the island?" She looked at Professor Hudson. "Is that safe?"

"If we all keep a proper situational awareness, it should be." Professor Hudson smiled. "I can assure you that neither the headmistress of our school or the headmaster of OAAS approve of an attrition-based educational model." She chuckled quietly.

Raine laughed. "I hope so." She stared at the forest in search of any other strange shadows but found only trees and the occasional bird. "Skimmers and mirror cats. Plants that can crawl. Musical fireflies. This place really is a magic island."

CHAPTER ELEVEN

"And I can't cut anything with a sword?" Adrien asked with a frown as he thrust some of the increasingly dense brush aside. He walked at the front of the group beside Professor Hudson. Despite the fact that the professor had told him earlier it was unnecessary, he held a long sword in his hand. "I can produce a machete if you think it would be more efficient."

"This isn't about efficiency, Adrien, and I'm sure the others told you the same thing on your trips with them." The professor shook her head. "Nothing permanent. Not at this stage of the survey."

Raine walked at the rear of the formation with Asher beside her. Finn remained in the center.

"I bet he's awesome to have in a fight," Asher murmured and gestured at the Light Elf. "I know he hasn't revealed too much of what it means to be a Guardian in our chats, but I can tell. He might be a little uptight, but he seems like the real deal. Kick-butt Light Elf warrior."

Raine nodded and kept her voice low as she responded.

"Yes. We've had our share of battles together—against creatures and people. Adrien is brave and selfless. He's also very skilled. I don't know if I would have made it out of some of our adventures without him."

Her companion's expression turned contemplative. "You've never wavered from your path, have you? Not only the Trouble Squad but you in particular."

"Huh? What do you mean?"

"Going into the FBI. It's like it's practically destiny." He shrugged. "Some Seer sat on Oriceran and recited quatrains about Quantico, probably."

"It's family tradition more than destiny." She looked up to watch a giant metallic purple caterpillar crawl up the side of a tree and wondered if it would become an equally impressive butterfly.

"But you didn't know you had magic before. Shouldn't that have changed things?"

Raine shook her head. "It only made me want to go into the FBI more, not less. They need people like me and William. They need all the magicals they can get in this crazy world. Having to face Eris only convinced me of that."

"I'm a little jealous."

She frowned and hoped this wasn't a segue into another question about her love life. "Jealous?"

"Of that kind of focus." Asher raised his hand and whispered an incantation. An image of a small black sheep appeared before it blew away with a breeze. "That's me. I come from a respectable family with a proud legacy, not only on Earth but also Oriceran, but I'm merely a goof at school. My parents don't mind, but I think they would love it if I came to them and said, 'I want to join the FBI and apprehend chaos witches.'"

Raine shook her head. "You're not merely a goof. You seem like you're the leader of your—I don't know, Mainer Monster Hunter Squad?"

"Mainer Monster Hunter Squad? I like that, but I also lucked into that."

"We all luck into our lives." She chuckled quietly. "It's not like we can choose where we're born and who our parents are."

The elf nodded and his normal easy smile returned. "True enough. What I mean, though, is that I'm not sure what I want to do with my life, and I admire that so many of you FBI Trouble Squad members know what you will do once you're out of school."

Finn yelped and launched into the air, a tight vine wound around his ankle. His wand slipped out of his hand and fell before he could even think to try to catch it.

Adrien spun toward the boy and gripped his sword tightly. "An enemy?"

Raine raised her wand but Professor Hudson sighed and shook her head.

The vine swayed back and forth. It stretched from a patch of glowing flowers nestled between three trees that grew close together.

"Get me down!" the wizard shouted and his face turned red, both from indignation and fear and the rush of blood to his head. "Before this thing eats me."

Adrien advanced, but the professor put her hand on his shoulder and shook her head firmly once again.

The elf frowned. "He's under attack, Professor. We have to help him."

"Again, it's the difference between deadly and merely inconvenient." The witch raised her wand and cast a shield spell around the boy. "This particular vine is simply a moving vine. It lacks the capability of eating anyone. This is basically an anti-predator defense. It will hold him for a few minutes and drop him. Normal animals will immediately flee thereafter."

"I don't care about being eaten," Finn shouted. "I'm getting dizzy."

Professor Hudson aimed her wand at the ground and chanted another quick spell. A large floating disc of light appeared beneath the boy. "Tickle it."

"Huh?"

"Tickle it." She gestured toward the vine. "That will force your release, and it will grow quiescent for long enough that we can leave the area without additional trouble."

"I can't believe this. I have to tickle a vine." He growled with real annoyance and grunted as he strained to reach his captor. Still muttering, he complied with the instruction and it dropped him almost instantly. The boy yelled as he fell but he landed on the professor's disc and bounced once. "That was so not cool."

Asher shrugged. "I'd consider giving it a whirl."

Raine retrieved Finn's wand from the undergrowth. She walked over to him and held it out. "Here you go."

Adrien waved his hand, and his sword disappeared. "You're right, Professor. A blade is unnecessary against an enemy we can tickle into submission."

The Wood Elf laughed.

Finn groaned, his chagrin visible on his face. "Make this sound cooler when you tell the others, please."

Raine smiled as she looked at the gleaming bushes directly ahead of her. She held her quick-transfer scroll up and pressed her thumb to a glyph. "Multi-colored bushes, about four feet in height, shimmering with no obvious external source. They have small round berries on them. Um…" She bit her lip as she drew a field guide from a wide cargo pocket. She somehow managed to flip awkwardly through it one-handed before she found a useful chart. "Oh…um, category A2-43 per the field guide." She jammed the booklet into the pocket before she removed her thumb from the scroll. "I wonder what they taste like."

"Sweet death," announced Professor Hudson as she walked into the clearing.

"Excuse me?" She frowned. "I didn't intend to eat one. I was simply curious."

The professor nodded at the bushes. "I'm not an expert like Professor Fowler or Professor Kaylis, but I'm not totally ignorant of such things either. These are pretty to look at, but those berries can be used in some fairly nasty potions, even beyond their inherent poisonous nature. You're worried about mirror cats, but always remember that not everything beautiful and magical is good. If you can take that knowledge away from this survey as well, it would be helpful."

Raine sighed and nodded. "So, this isn't a new species?"

Professor Hudson shook her head. "You've asked that before, but keep in mind that the point of the survey isn't to find new species so much as to establish which species are here. It'd be more convenient in many ways if there were fewer unknown species. That would mean it'll be easier to manage and decide on the disposition of this island and the creatures living on it in the long run, even if that's not something our group will have to worry about."

"I know." Raine smiled sheepishly. "But it would be nice if I could find some crazy bird and name it Campbell's Raptor or something like that."

Asher, Finn, and Adrien returned from their examinations of other plants and animals nearby. They rolled their scrolls and tucked them into pockets.

The Light Elf pointed toward some shadows in the distance. "There's a large group of aquaboars over there eating nuts and berries."

Professor Hudson nodded. "We'll go around them. They won't bother us if we don't bother them."

A pulse of magic passed through the area and the group exchanged wary glances.

"Uh oh," Raine muttered.

In the next instant, the ground shook beneath their feet. The trees around them writhed as the earth convulsed. Being a moving plant wasn't only limited to ticklish vines anymore, but the bigger concern was the dozens of squeals in the distance.

The professor held her wand level, her face tight. "Everyone, get ready to cast." She looked at Adrien. "Avoidance, not battle."

He nodded without hesitation. "Understood." A genuine

smile appeared. "I haven't played all that Louper without mastering avoiding dangers quickly."

A chorus of squeals joined with the rumble of heavy hoofbeats and cracking branches. The dark forms in the distance grew more defined and left little doubt—the aquaboars had plunged instinctively into a panicked stampede. Unfortunately, they'd chosen the group's direction for their headlong rush.

The ground continued to shudder, which stirred the creatures into greater urgency.

Adrien pointed his hands down and cast a burst spell. He elevated and caught hold of a jerking branch. Finn grinned and mirrored his maneuver.

Asher raised his hand and chanted a spell. A branch extended toward him, and he grabbed it with both hands as it pulled him up.

The stampeding aquaboars, their dark blue hides now more discernable, continued their loud rampage. The earthquake ceased, but the animals now moved with mindless instinct and were unlikely to slow or turn from their current course.

Raine followed the Louper players' example and scrambled up a tree. She eased to a sitting position atop a thick branch.

Professor Hudson raised her wand in front of her face and a glowing ramp appeared.

"Okay, that's one way to do it," Raine said, impressed despite her heart-thudding trepidation.

The front line of the stampeding herd passed beneath the students and the animals made no effort to avoid the gleaming translucent ramp. Instead, they simply raced over it and jumped off as if they'd all decided to take up boar parkour. The witch stood quietly, her expression serene, as beast after beast leapt over her.

Adrien's branch snapped, and his eyes widened in surprise as he fell. Finn shouted a spell, and a rope extended from his wand and wound around the elf. With a groan, he hauled Adrien up to his branch.

"Did you like that one, bro?" the wizard asked with a grin. "I wanted to save it for next season and use it to surprise a few players."

Adrien grinned, his relief evident. "I appreciate the save and the preview."

Finn raised his hand for a high-five. The Light Elf hesitated for a moment before he struck his rescuer's hand.

The last group of aquaboars passed beneath their perches. Professor Hudson remained untouched as the dark blue mass continued into the forest.

She looked up. "It seems everyone remains unhurt?"

Adrien nodded. "Thanks to Finn."

Asher exhaled a sharp breath. "I feel like this was revenge for the fact that I like bacon."

Raine laughed. "Maybe."

"Meat preferences aside," the professor said, "we should get going."

CHAPTER TWELVE

Raine sat on a large rock and stared at the beach, Cameron beside her, and a soft smile touched both their faces. The sun hung low in the sky, but there was still an hour or so before sunset. Without a watch, phone, or clocks, she had reverted to more basic rhythms. Individual minutes and hours seemed abstract and less important than the main events of the day—dawn, noon, sunset, and the coming of night. It might be too much to say she was in touch with her ancient ancestors, but she at least could start to appreciate what life was like before smartphones.

There was a certain taunting irritation to sitting in front of an ocean they weren't allowed to swim in. Although they hadn't confirmed the presence of anything other than skimmers and a few other minor sea creatures, all the professors agreed that there was a real danger of serious injury should the students swim in the ocean and possibly encounter a magical sea monster. For now, they'd forbidden anything other than a little splashing near the shore.

The last few days had passed without serious incident, either tremors or animal-related. To her continued disappointment, their surveys failed to identify any new species, but their cataloging had proceeded well, and their work would benefit the Magical Multitudes Project. Although they were focused primarily on large land plants and animals for their particular task and captured only a small amount of the island's total biodiversity, she felt enormously satisfied every time she returned to camp and transferred her notes into Professor Tarelli's book. It was rare that she could contribute to expanding the bounds of knowledge.

"It's relaxing here," Raine said with a smile. "I know we're doing all this survey work, but I almost feel like it's a big vacation. I know this isn't the most romantic beach in the world, and it'll slice our feet if we tried to run around barefoot, but it's still nice. I'm so used to spending all my time in cities during the summer."

Cameron nodded. "I always like to get back to nature. It's hard not to when you're a shifter. It helps give me perspective.

"Is that what I need? Perspective."

"That's part of your problem, Raine. Sometimes, you simply need to put the brakes on and think of something other than the FBI. It's good to have goals, but you have to recharge the batteries every now and again."

Kelly, Asher, Adrien, and Finn stood in the distance and chatted excitedly about something. Whatever it was involved grand gestures and pointing up and down the beach.

When Raine had last seen Philip, Sara, William, and Evie, they'd claimed they wanted to check a few things in the forest. Both couples conveniently examined separate areas. She didn't press them on the details because she didn't want to have to lie to the professors, and if she wasn't sure where the students were, it made that part easy.

"It's hard not to be focused when I want it so badly, and it's so close. What seemed like a distant destination I would never reach is now coming soon. Very soon. I'm worried about screwing it up." She smiled as a skimmer poked through the surface in the distance. "But taking a while to think about it and reflect on it is nice, too." She blew out a breath. "And it's been nice getting to know the students from Orono. I wasn't sure if I'd like them, but they're all pleasant in their own way. It's been interesting to learn how a different magical school works."

A brief, uncomfortable look passed over Cameron's face before he replaced it with a blank expression and chased that away with a smile. "It's funny. I didn't know if I would feel safe here, but that's really stupid considering that I go home all the time where we don't have wards and professors guarding us. The whole mysterious magical island thing made me worry about more deadly creatures, but we've barely run into any. I know there are some, but if we never see them, it's hard to worry."

"I never feel unsafe away from the school. I only miss it —and my friends." Raine rested her head on Cameron's shoulder. "And you, even if Uncle Jerry's been cool about letting you spend time with us. I wish I could stay with you and your pack for a while, but there's no way he'll allow that."

Adrien, Kelly, Asher, and Finn all vaulted the rock wall and rushed toward the camp in a hurry.

"I wonder what's going on?" She frowned. "Trouble?"

Cameron shrugged. "If it was something important, they would have done something to draw our attention. You know, it's not always up to you to be first in and last out."

"I only want to do my part to help others."

He ruffled her hair. "I know, and I'm not saying you should change. That dedication to helping others is one of the things I love about you, but I worry about you too."

Raine sighed. "I know, but I can't help it. And I feel bad every time I make you worry, but I don't think I'll ever change. I'm not the kind of girl who will be satisfied to sit back when someone else is in trouble."

The couple fell into silence and lingered a while to simply rest and watch the ocean for several minutes. Adrien and the Orono students returned smiling with Professors Hudson, Kaylis, and Powell behind them, all with their wands out.

"Okay, I definitely want to know what's going on now." She straightened and searched the horizon for any marine threats, but even the skimmer was gone.

The professors raised their wands. A slight grinding noise issued into the silence as rocks rose from the nearby beach and parts of the rock wall. The stones floated toward the beach and came together to form rough platforms. Other material coalesced into tall rock columns from which other small platforms grew to connect the pillars.

Raine stood and stared as this magical sculptural work continued. The purpose didn't seem to be to create a building. Or, if it was, it was the bare skeleton of one, but the spacing of the platforms suggested otherwise.

Cameron stood and shook his head. "I have no idea what this is, but it doesn't look like it's anything involving danger. Maybe they're making a monument to our greatness?" He smirked.

"I doubt that." She stood and jogged toward Adrien when curiosity overwhelmed her.

The elf watched the professors' work with a slight smile on his face. He nodded every few seconds and his head turned toward Raine as she approached.

"Hello, Raine," he said.

"What's going on?"

He gestured to the airborne rocks. "I was discussing Louper with Finn and we shared a little about strategies and experiences. We obviously don't have the gear or facilities to play it here or even the teams, but we were bored, so we decided to come up with our own game—or a prototype of one, at least. It's not exactly Louper, but it should provide some entertainment."

The shifter frowned as he stopped beside them. "A prototype game?"

Adrien nodded. "We're calling it mazeball. Professor Hudson will transmute plant material into a nice ball for us after they finish putting our course together. They have to reinforce it so it can take the tremors. I'm surprised it didn't take more convincing."

"So am I." Raine couldn't help wondering if the professors weren't bored as well.

"We'll start the game as a three-on-three match." The elf pointed at the top of the structure. "There will be four baskets, two at the top and two at the bottom of four multi-level courts. It's simple. For now, we'll simply say that whichever team gets to ten points first wins. You score by getting the ball into the basket, but no floating the ball with direct magic is allowed. That would make things too easy."

He pointed at Finn. "You can't directly restrain or attack another player, but you can put up obstacles on the platforms." He shrugged. "It's not simulated, so we need to be more careful. We can't have everyone hurling fireballs." He looked at Cameron with a wide grin. "The professors still insist that everyone play with shields on. We'll provide you with one if you want to play. All we need is to break falls."

The shifter studied the court speculatively. "I might give it a shot."

Kelp flowed from the ocean into the air and danced to Professor Hudson's moving wand like she was the conductor of a silent orchestra. The seaweed separated and wove itself to form a net at the bottom of the stone columns and platforms that made up the mazeball court. Additional nets began to form around the sides.

Adrien pointed at the Orono students he'd spoken to earlier. "We have three there with Asher, Finn, and Kelly. Would you two join me for our test run after the professors finish setting up the course? We're not saying all the games have to be Charlottesville versus Orono, but we still have some aspects to work out so might as well start our first test match."

She smiled. "Sure. Why not?"

The finished course might have lacked the aesthetic elegance of something prepared with more time and attention to detail, but it would serve its practical purpose of prototyping their new sport. Without relying on floating magic, the court had a four-by-four-by-four grid of platforms connected to columns. Baskets hung on the center top and bottom platforms on both sides. Dense netting surrounded the outside and the bottom to catch players and rogue balls.

There was more than sufficient space for the teams to move between the platforms, but it was difficult to move up without a running jump. Burst spells or magic that created some sort of line were practically a necessity.

That reality inconvenienced Cameron, but he didn't mind as he focused on mostly patrolling the bottom level in the first minutes of their match. An occasion shift into wolf form and a run with a mid-air shift into his human form allowed him a quick transition above when necessary.

Adrien clutched the white ball beneath his arm. It was smaller than a soccer ball but still much larger than a softball. Two small handles projected from either side. The unfavorable aerodynamics meant it wouldn't go far if thrown, but that suited the tight quarters of the enclosed mazeball court perfectly.

Taking an object to a target instead of the target being the final destination required a little more adjustment than

Adrien had anticipated. He passed the ball with a quick throw to Cameron, who caught it with ease and rushed toward the lower goal.

Kelly raised her wand with a grin and uttered a spell. A thin layer of oil appeared on the platform seconds before the shifter landed on it. He took wolf form and closed his jaws on one of the handles before he bounded to the next platform, his paws slick with oil. The idea was good, but he skidded and fell off the edge into the net with a growl of frustration.

Cameron shifted and shook out his oily hands. "Uh, do we count that as out of bounds?"

"I think so," Finn called from above. "It's one thing if the ball falls, but if your entire body falls, it should count."

He hopped onto the platform and lobbed the ball to Kelly. "I won't fall for that again."

"We'll see." She waggled her eyebrows.

Raine tucked the small ball under her arm as she leapt to the lower platform. Adrien remained high, but Cameron was near the lower goal. She tossed the ball to the side.

Kelly laughed. "Come on, Raine, don't give up."

She grinned at the other witch's taunt, pointed her wand, and rattled off her spell. While she might not be able to put together a complicated court with ease like the professors, that didn't mean she couldn't manipulate the environment with her magic. She'd learned more than only shields and invisibility in her three years at the School of Necessary Magic.

A thin stone slab projected from one of the platforms. The ball struck it squarely and bounced off at an angle to rocket toward Cameron.

Asher grinned, dropped off the side, and grasped one of the lower platforms without the aid of magic. "Good play, Raine. We didn't even think of doing that sort of thing."

The shifter caught the ball, spun, and bounded over a muddy pool near the bottom hoop. He thunked it into the basket and pumped his fist. "Now we're tied again at five to five."

Finn clapped. "Nice. Very nice."

Kelly threw her wand in the air and let it spin a few times before she caught it. "Will we allow that? Altering the course in such a big way? I know we decided on one trap per platform unless you clear it, but this new strategy makes it an entirely different game."

Adrien shrugged. "I can see the practical issues in cleaning the course up, but I like it, even if I hadn't anticipated that play style. For a game we made up, it still feels very engaging. More so, in some ways."

Finn nodded. "I do too. It makes it more strategic. It feels like the play would flow better with four or five players, but this is still great fun."

Raine stared at her creation for a few seconds. "We should establish the rule that it has to extend from the court rather than hanging in the air. That makes it safer and means people can plan better. And also, no matter what, there has to be at least one path to the goal. Otherwise, people will simply throw walls up all around it."

Asher nodded. "That sounds sensible."

The other players nodded their agreement.

Cameron picked the ball up and tossed it to the Wood Elf, who moved to a center back platform. They'd collectively decided that these areas would be the starting position for each round.

Asher elevated with a quick burst spell and threw the ball to a waiting Kelly. Adrien lingered near the goal. The witch took the ball and pitched it to her side. A spell created a new wall to bounce off, but her grin faded when Adrien summoned an ice wall in her path. The ball bounced off the ice and fell over the edge where a waiting Raine caught it and threw it immediately to Cameron.

The off-balanced Orono team didn't even have time to release a spell before the boy careened to the other goal and dunked the ball.

"Six to five." The shifter bowed. "Maybe I should have taken up Louper, too."

"Yes, you should have," Adrien called from above. "It's fun."

Cameron threw the ball to Finn. "But don't get me wrong. I know you and Adrien would destroy me in Louper."

Finn grinned. "Probably, but this game isn't over yet."

Raine took several deep breaths and wiped the sweat off her brow. Her innovations in gameplay had been exciting, but they'd also created a far more defensively-minded game, which relied as much on eliminating obstacles as generating them. The game now truly lived up to the name mazeball.

The teams had fought to a nine-nine tie, and both sides decided, for the premiere game, that ten would be sufficient. Once they had established the rules more firmly, they would consider adding a requirement that a team needed to be ahead by two points to win at the end.

Several walls now covered the court at different angles. The teams had a brief discussion as to whether they should reset the course after every point, but they decided that part of the fun of their new game was reacting to the ever-changing court.

Raine lowered her wand, burst up, and managed to avoid a trip snare Finn had cast on the platform directly in front of her. She spun and threw the ball toward Adrien. He elevated quickly with a burst at the same time that Asher summoned a wall.

The Wood Elf winced as his opponent slammed into the new wall, but the player only emitted a quiet grunt and his shield took the brunt of the punishment. He seized the top and flipped over the barrier, a slight trail of blood trickling down his face, and snatched the falling ball. Another burst careened him toward the almost completely blocked goal basket.

Asher raised his hands to cast another spell. Two of the walls collapsed around the goal, and a new one rose in front of Adrien, but the Light Elf vaulted off the top of the new obstacle for his final delivery of the ball into the basket.

He landed with a grin and wiped the blood off the side of his face. "We have a few things to work out, but so far, I like it. It's not quite Louper, but it's still fun."

Asher clapped and Finn and Kelly soon joined him.

"Good job, guys," the Wood Elf said. "Now, we need everyone else to play."

CHAPTER THIRTEEN

Mazeball was far from Raine's mind as she trudged through the western forest with Cameron, Sara, Philip, and Dnai. The professors had decided that the students had all demonstrated enough awareness of the dangers of the island and control of their boats that they could now venture into the woods without an adult.

It wasn't that the adults left all the work to the students. Some groups performed their daily surveys with a professor. Some didn't, but the change in requirements allowed them to cover more ground.

The loud flapping of Dnai's wings sounded from above as she flew to a new branch. "I never thought I'd spend a summer flying around cataloging magical animals. It's actually more interesting than I thought it might be."

Raine laughed. "I never even thought I would end up in a magic school."

Philip squatted near some colorful toadstools that were a foot in diameter. He recorded their features on his scroll before he shook his head. "Do you know what this whole experience has taught me?"

Sara shook her head. "What?"

"I'm a city boy through and through." He stood with a grin. "Sure, it's relaxing and all, but I'd kill for a good movie night about now."

Raine walked forward to inspect a nest in some low-hanging branches. It was a simple sparrow's nest—interesting but a little disappointing. "What movie will you have us watch next?"

"Did you ever see the *Breakfast Club?*" he asked.

His companions shook their head.

"What's a breakfast club?" Cameron asked. "Is it some sort of drama about a group of people who sit around discussing politics over breakfast? It sounds seriously boring."

"It's a teen drama. High-school stuff, and it's way old. The made it all the way back in the eighties." The wizard shrugged. "It's about these high-school kids who get in trouble, so they all have to serve detention, and they're all different personalities. One guy's a jock and one girl is basically the princess of the school. There's also a bad boy, a smart kid, and a weird girl. It's really dated and stuff in many ways. It's pre-gate, and they don't do much with computers, let alone magic, and no one has a smartphone. At one point, it's supposed to be weird that a girl's eating sushi."

Cameron craned his neck to watch a colorful bird with three wings flying overhead. They'd cataloged the species a week before. "If it's so dated, why do you want to watch it?"

"Because it's still relatable, dude. They learn how much they have in common as they spend time together talking about stuff. Well, that and a few other things, but the main point is the talking and learning that they might be different, but they can still understand each other." Philip licked his lips. "They're not magicals, but they reminded me of the Trouble Squad when we first started. We were all from different backgrounds and cared about different things. We each had problems, regardless of our backgrounds, but we came together and made a difference. It's strange how a sixty-year-old pre-gate movie can still feel relevant."

Dnai flapped to a new branch. "Our group was like that, too. All different, but we became good friends."

Cameron grinned. "So I'm the bad boy in this movie, right?"

"I suppose." Philip smiled sheepishly. "I'm the nerd. Adrien's the jock, obviously."

Raine laughed. "Who am I then?"

Cameron smirked. "The princess."

Sara, Philip, and Dnai all laughed.

"How am I the princess? I don't come from some distinguished line of witches like Josephine." Raine put her hands on her hips and challenged them with her best defiant face.

"Because you're a good girl whom the teachers and library gnomes all love?" The shifter's smirk only grew wider. "Nothing will be a perfect match."

Sara eyed Philip warningly. "If you say I'm the weird girl, I'll tie you up in vines."

He grinned but wisely remained silent.

Dnai fluttered to the ground. "It sounds like it fits my

circle a little tighter in some ways." She cocked her head cheekily. "I think I'm the weird girl."

Philip raised a hand placatingly. "It's like Cameron said. Not everything will be a perfect fit. The point is that it reminded me of how we came together and made each other better. To be honest, I wasn't always the best guy when school started." His shoulders slumped. "I made a lot of mistakes, and I would have understood if you guys didn't want to hang out with me anymore after some of the stunts I pulled."

Cameron clapped him on the shoulder. "We all made mistakes." His gaze flicked to Raine. "Even when they involved running off without getting the help a person needed."

Raine's cheeks heated. She opened her mouth but closed it when two humanoid shadows passed in the distance and pointed her wand that way. "I saw something. It might be mirror cats, but it might be something else."

"If I had any idea what a mirror cat scent smells like, I'd track them, but we should at least investigate." He shifted and gestured with his muzzle.

The students crept forward and followed her direction, their wands at the ready, except for Dnai who held a hand up. They all summoned shields, and Raine layered one over Cameron.

She took long, deep breaths to steady her sudden thrill of excitement as they walked through the trees toward the where she had seen the shadows. They finally reached a few huge trunks where two dark humanoid shadows stood. One had the outline of wings on its back.

"Okay, that's weird," Philip muttered. He raised his palm. "Uh, we mean you no harm?"

"Remember," Raine murmured. "Whatever happens, we can't hurt them."

"I'm more worried about them hurting us."

Sara's hand drifted toward a belt pouch filled with seeds and berries.

A third shadow drifted in from the side. All three shapes twisted and rippled. Three large, bright white cats replaced them, razor-sharp teeth in their wide mouths. The red-eyed felines snarled and crept forward.

Cameron stood in front of Raine and growled. The creatures paused but crouched, ready to pounce.

Raine fought to slow her thudding heart. "Definitely mirror cats." She backed away slowly. "They aren't intelligent, right?"

Dnai shuffled quietly in retreat without moving her eyes from the animals. "Nope. Darn. If I fly now, it'll probably spook them."

Sara fished a handful of seeds and berries out of her pouch. "Are they stronger than normal big cats?"

The Arpak shook her head. "They're strong and they can claw you and bite you, but they aren't any tougher than a jaguar or something like that. The shadow illusions are the tricky part. That's how they corner prey."

"Cameron, shift into human form," Raine murmured.

He turned and cocked his head.

"Please. It'll be hard for you not to hurt them as a wolf."

He transformed and scowled unhappily. The mirror cats retreated hastily with another snarl.

"I don't know if that helped or not, but we have to consider our safety, too." The shifter frowned.

Raine shook her head. "We'll be fine. They can't shred through shields, right?" Uncertainty crept into her voice as she looked at Dnai.

The other girl shrugged. "Not that I know of, but it's not like I've fought one. They do have a really good sense of smell, though. That's what Professor Tarelli said. Their big thing is misdirection."

Sara narrowed her eyes and several seeds and berries held between her fingers had begun to grow. "I'll tie them up so we can run. If there's no professor here, we shouldn't keep this confrontation up."

Cameron nodded. "I think that's a wise plan."

"Okay, on five, four, three, two, one." She flung her tiny missiles.

Dnai vaulted upward as the others turned to run.

The mirror cats growled and charged. Vines erupted from where the seeds and the berries had popped and released a thick pink mist. The felines bounded forward but soon lay entangled in a thick mass of vines, their hides half-dyed pink.

The students rushed through the trees in the direction of the shore where they'd tied their boat up. They'd barely managed a few yards before another humanoid shadow stepped out of the trees and transformed into a mirror cat.

Raine fired a restraint spell within a second. A thick rope appeared and twirled to wind around the feline. It snarled and growled as its claws ripped into the rope, but the delay gave Sara enough time to bind it with her vines.

The survey team ran on and Dnai circled a few times

overhead to keep pace with them. Low-hanging branches whipped at their faces, but their shields protected them from scratches.

Raine's heart galloped in her chest. She glanced constantly over her shoulder for signs of pursuit.

Sara was the first to slow from a sprint to a mere jog, followed by Philip. Raine and Cameron slowed, and Dnai landed.

Philip peered nervously into the forest. "I think we lost them for now."

"We could have taken them." Cameron seemed disgruntled. "It's not like we were hunting them. It would have been self-defense."

"Well, we didn't get hurt and we didn't hurt them." Raine shrugged. "I think that's a win. Let's get back to camp. The professors can figure out how they want to handle it." She found it difficult to look away from the trees, though, and while her heart slowed, it still beat harder than normal. The encounter had been way too close.

CHAPTER FOURTEEN

Professor Tarelli seemed fully attentive as she stared at Raine with her wide yellow eyes. "Interesting, Sophia. Very interesting."

"That's Raine, Professor."

"It's not raining."

"No, my name." She sighed.

The students had beat a retreat to their boat and returned to camp, where they waited at the firepit. No one else was present, and it was a couple of hours before Professors Tarelli and Powell both arrived at the same time. Neither had escorted a group of students that afternoon.

"Oh, yes, of course." The professor shook her head. "I'll get it eventually. Keep reminding me."

Professor Powell rubbed his chin. He looked at Raine and her group. "None of you seem the worse for wear."

She gestured to Sara. "She disabled the mirror cats, and we ran."

"Good!" Professor Tarelli shouted and immediately

frowned. "I'm sorry," she said more quietly. "I'm pleased you didn't panic and harm the creatures. They are very rare, even on Oriceran. With your capabilities, you could easily have killed them, and I appreciate your restraint despite the difficult and challenging situation."

Cameron stepped forward and pointed at the boat. "Okay, so we were able to disable them and run, but that doesn't change the fact there are hungry mirror cats in that area. I understand that we don't want to kill anything on the island, but we can't always retreat."

"True," Professor Powell said. "And no one expects you to do something like that either."

"Meaning what?" The shifter folded his arms over his chest and his frustration all but radiated off him. "I don't have fancy restraining magic, but I won't stand by and let some animal tear Raine—tear anyone apart." His nostrils flared.

"Calm down, Cameron." The professor pointed his wand at the forest. "The point is that we don't send you into the forest at random. You check particular areas, and we record data related to this systematic search. Now we know that the area you checked today has mirror cats. They maintain a limited range." He glanced at Professor Tarelli. "Correct?"

She nodded once.

"So we'll only need to be careful around that general area," he continued, "and we'll make sure any groups working there—or near there—have a professor with them. If necessary, we'll put the cats to sleep while we do our work for a given day. The important thing is that you didn't panic. Not that I'd expect you to." He smiled at the students from his school. "You've all had to deal with far more danger to your lives than I did by your age. You're more seasoned than some junior PDA agents at this point, I suspect." He turned and nodded to Dnai. "And considering some of the creatures I've heard you and your friends have handled, I'm hardly surprised you didn't panic."

The Arpak girl grinned. "It helps when you can fly, even if it's hard for me to get above the canopy when we explore the interior of the island."

Professor Tarelli extended her hand. "Please give me your scrolls. I need to transfer the information you found. We'll leave that area alone for a few days. It'll allow the mirror cats some chance to relax. We don't want them to think we're aggressively invading their territory."

The students retrieved their scrolls and handed them to her. She hurried off toward her cabin, mumbling under her breath about data accuracy.

Professor Powell smiled. "We're still waiting for everyone else. Stick close to the camp, but there's nothing else you need to do for the moment."

Cameron grabbed Raine's hand. "Come with me."

She blinked and looked over her shoulder at Sara, who simply shrugged as he led her away from the firepit and cabins and toward the mazeball court. She tugged her hand away gently and followed him, confused.

He stopped a few yards from the court, turned to face her, and folded his arms. "Aren't you angry at all?"

"Angry?" She shook her head. "Why would I be angry?"

"I don't know. I just..." He gritted his teeth. "It's one thing when we're in danger because we've been dragged into some sort of weird adventure against a tutorial faerie who has come to life or crazed assassins or chaos witches. But this is supposed to be a school trip, and they act like it's unimportant that we got attacked."

"No one was hurt." Raine pulled her wand off her belt and held it up. "And the truth is, I don't think we were really in danger. This is why they wanted juniors, Cameron. We know how to handle ourselves. Even if we weren't the FBI Trouble Squad, we'd know the kinds of spells we need to protect ourselves without killing anything."

Cameron averted his gaze. "You do."

"Yes, we do."

The shifter shook his head. "No, you do. I don't know."

"I don't understand."

"It's..." He dragged in a deep breath and let it out slowly. "No one ever treats me differently. You—and all of them, really—were nice to me from the beginning, but it's times like this when I remember that I'm not like you all. I can't do magic. The only way I can defend you is by shifting and shredding a mirror cat before it hurts you, and I don't—" His hands curled into fists. "I don't like thinking that's all I'm good for."

She slipped her wand onto her belt and wrapped her arms around him. "Don't ever think like that. Just because you can't cast restraining spells doesn't mean anything." She smiled with gentle reassurance. "You've been off since we got here, though. Is that what it is? I don't understand it. It's not like the Orono students have anything against you because you're a shifter."

"I'm..." Cameron growled his frustration. "Sometimes, I wonder if a shifter's the best boyfriend for a witch."

Raine snorted. "That's not how love and relationships work. I love you for who you are. I don't push you aside because you're a shifter. I fell in love with everything about you as a person. Being a shifter is part of who you are, so since I love you, that means I love that part of you."

"You've never thought about being with someone else?" She stared into his eyes, which flashed yellow. "Someone with actual magic?"

She shook her head firmly. "Why would I need someone else when I have you?" She pressed her forehead against his. "What is this really about? Where is it coming from? You can't be that upset because you couldn't restrain those mirror cats."

"I see the way Asher keeps looking at you," he muttered.

Raine sighed and pulled away. "And I've already made it a hundred percent clear to him that I already have a boyfriend. He hasn't bothered me about it since. You don't need to be jealous. I don't love Asher. I love you." She glanced over her shoulder to ensure that the professors were out of sight before she gave him a soft kiss. "Okay?"

"Okay," he grumbled and blushed. "It's hard to be a wolf shifter. I'm territorial about everything, and I can't help it. You're one of the best things to ever happen to me, and I keep thinking I'll lose you—if not to the job, then to someone else."

"Not if I can help it." She smiled and slid her arm around him. "Professor Powell said there wasn't anything we needed to do. We might as well take a little walk up the beach. There are far fewer rocks on it since they built the mazeball court."

He chuckled. "Okay, let's go."

CHAPTER FIFTEEN

Sara waved her arms as she jumped down to the first level of platforms. "I'm open. I'm open."

Today's match featured Sara, Josephine, and Kelly versus Heidi, Asher, and Adrien. No one had really kept particular track of wins versus losses, and since there were no permanent teams, there wasn't much reason to. As competitive as some of the students could be, the point of the game was basically fun, nothing more.

Josephine hurled the ball against a nearby raised wall. It struck and bounced to another wall she had conjured a few minutes prior and then another, like a game of 3D pinball. The kitsune caught it with a grin and raced around the spinning pole Heidi had summoned earlier in the match.

She had taken several steps before a stone wall raised in front of her. A quick upward glance confirmed that Adrien stood one level above, his hands out and his eyes narrowed.

Sara didn't try to vault over the obstacle or move around. Instead, she decided it was time for the application of conventional sports tactics. She clutched the ball with both hands and leapt up to arc it through the air in a comfortable jump shot. The topspin of the handled ball brought it down quickly, and it struck the edge of the basket and bounced a few times before it fell inside.

"Woo!" She raised her arms in victory. "We take the lead, four to three." She waved at Adrien. "Fear my jump shot." Her smile wavered when he simply stared at her. "Or did we want to make it the rule that you have to dunk?"

The elf shrugged. "We can talk about that after the match. Let's see how it plays out first. It's harder for most of the players to do that because they have to hold their wands with one hand, so it might be unfair for people like us who don't need wands."

Josephine looked at her white wand, her expression neutral. "Not all challenges have to be easily balanced. I don't mind either call."

Asher grinned. "I can see it both ways."

Cameron, who watched the match along with several others from outside the court, nodded. "If we can take more shots like that and you don't block the top, it might end up a very short game. Just saying."

Raine nodded. "I like the idea of having to go to the basket to score."

"Oh, well." Adrien jumped a few platforms down to recover the ball. "By the time the summer is over, I'm sure we'll have worked out equitable and reasonable rules. If not, there's always Louper. Now, it's time to—" His eyes widened, and he stiffened instinctively.

Every student felt the pulse of magic. They understood what it meant, even if it had been days since the last earthquake. The mazeball players dropped into the outer net at the first tremor.

The ground shook violently. Trees swayed in the distance, and the stone columns groaned with the motion of the earth.

Raine and other spectators stood hastily and raced away from the court. The players pushed through the gaps in the outer net and sprinted down the beach after their friends.

Although they had all felt several earthquakes on the island, this time, the shifting earth flung Raine off her feet. Cameron scooped her up and continued to run. Sara and the other players bolted ahead of them.

A cacophony of flutters, growls, and squawks issued from the forest. Hundreds of birds burst from the trees into the sky.

Cameron stumbled but righted himself, Raine still in his arms. Loud crashes from the forest signaled that a few trees had lost their struggle against the seismic activity and toppled to their final end.

The tremor finally stopped and everyone looked around slowly to ensure that nothing had fallen on anyone.

Cameron set Raine down gently. "Are you okay?"

She nodded. "I'm fine. But that one was a lot stronger than any of the others we've felt on the island."

Adrien turned and studied the court intently. "I have to say I'm rather impressed. I see a few cracks here and there, but it survived a major earthquake. I have to congratulate the professors on their workmanship."

Sara shook her head. "But I'm not so sure I want to

depend on it holding up in the middle of another earthquake."

Professor Powell appeared near the top of the rock wall. He surveyed the beach, his expression somber. "Is everyone accounted for here?"

Raine nodded as she took stock of their surroundings. "Yes, Professor. Everyone was either playing mazeball or watching it."

He glanced at the court with a slight frown. "That earthquake was definitely stronger than the last few. I think it's best if we avoid mazeball for a while. It's too risky."

Asher groaned. "Seriously? But we're starting to figure it all out."

The professor shook his head decisively. "Until we have a better idea of what's causing the quakes, we won't be able to predict them." He gestured toward the structure. "We'll leave it for now. It might be that we get to the bottom of this sooner rather than later."

An hour later, the professors stood huddled in Basil's cabin.

Xander frowned. "We might have to consider with-drawing from the island early."

"We're making such great progress here." The other man shook his head. "No student has been hurt. If we don't let them play their little game, they'll be fine."

Tarelli nodded agreement. "Both groups of students are

very thorough, and I'm impressed with their work. I feel like we have a good momentum going."

Eleanor frowned and folded her arms, her expression uneasy. "But the earthquake was definitely stronger. It implies that next time, it could be even stronger."

Basil breathed deeply a few times and maintained a calm expression, although he seemed a little irritated. "No one's denying that, Eleanor, but we also aren't in the middle of New York, and we have no proof that it will get significantly stronger. Other than a smattering of cabins, the students' court, and the dock, there aren't any real structures here. A severe earthquake merely risks collapsing a few small buildings we could repair in hours, nothing more."

She pointed toward the door. "Trees fell last time. If we're out in the field, that's a risk."

"One that a shield or cutting spell can handle." He chuckled. "Let's be honest, given the kind of challenges both your students and our students have faced, I think it's entirely unnecessary to run from the island over a few minor earthquakes."

Xander stared at the other professor, his gaze penetrating. "This isn't about the bravery of the students. This is about making sure they're not hurt by something we and they have no ability to control."

Tarelli ran a hand over her smooth scalp and nibbled her lip. "The fact that it's getting worse is less reason to leave."

"What makes you say that?"

"We're close to finding something out. That's what I think. Isn't that why we're here? To learn things?"

He shrugged. "We're not a geology team. We're a zoological and botanical survey project."

"Great discoveries often are found by those who least expect it." She gasped. "Don't you think the students would love to be involved in a great discovery? It could be something they talk about for the rest of their lives."

"I suppose, but we have no certainty that will be the case." Eleanor pursed her lips.

"We have no certainty of anything." Tarelli looked down, frowning in thought. "Or it might be nothing but a coincidence, but I do fear that if we flee now, we'll teach our students to be overly cautious. In this age, I don't know if that is a virtue."

"I suppose we can see what happens," Xander conceded but with obvious reluctance. "If the earthquakes continue to worsen, though, we'll need to consider leaving, even if it means we get in those rowboats and steer all the way back to the mainland."

Basil smiled. "Of course. Of course. That all sounds quite reasonable, but I'm sure the earthquakes will turn out to be nothing."

Xander scoffed and shook his head. "Sorry, Basil. I stopped believing in idle hope a long time ago."

CHAPTER SIXTEEN

Raine inhaled deeply and savored the sweet aroma of the grilled pineapple before she bit into it. She wasn't sure where the professors had obtained the food because they weren't on a tropical island and they hadn't eaten any pineapple in their weeks on the island.

The Orono students had said Professor Kaylis couldn't cook, but whatever his other skills when it came to food preparation, the man could grill a delicious slice of fruit. He also—very noticeably—didn't cook anything else. Instead, he left the kebabs everyone had for their main course to Professor Powell as part of a little party treat for the students to mark the halfway point of their summer research trip to New Firefly Island.

Most of the students now lay on blankets on the beach and stared at the stars. Raine suspected the truth was that the professors felt bad about canceling mazeball, especially since there hadn't been new earthquakes for a week. With the Fourth of July coming up in a few days, that would have been a more logical time for an impromptu party, but she definitely wouldn't complain about having a little extra fun. She doubted that they were worried about offending Adrien's French sensibilities given that they had already told the students to consider different spells for their own fireworks display.

Evie sighed contently beside William. "I miss my family and working on potions, but I'm also really, really calm. Who knew surveying magical species could be so Zen?"

She glanced at the half-Ifrit. His eyes were closed, and his chest rose and fell lightly.

"Cameron and I talked about that a while ago," Raine said. "I've used my summers for mostly training for years now. Ironically, I'm doing less work despite working on this project. I think it's mostly that this has a feeling like summer camp when you think about it. With less singing and more magic. That, and more weird creatures."

The shifter turned to her with a smile but remained quiet.

"Summer camp, huh?" Evie said. "You're right. I never really did anything like this when I was younger. Maybe that's why I'm enjoying it so much."

"Probably," Raine said. "We're not slaves to a schedule."

Cameron nudged her. "Don't oversell it, Raine."

"I'm just saying, is all. You're the one who told me I obsess over the FBI."

"True enough, but you love normal school, too."

She nodded. "I'm not saying I don't, only that I like this, too. If it weren't for the stupid earthquakes, this would have been even more relaxing."

Asher rested on his own blanket, his fingers laced behind his head. "I'm like you guys. My summers are usually super-busy. I'm always focused on improving my magic because my parents expect it. Even if they don't have a particular job I have to do, they are obsessed with carrying on the family magical legacy." He chuckled. "Not that I mind too much, but that might be why I like to kick back more at school and goof off. You, know, to appreciate my magic as something other than part of a legacy."

"There are many social obligations my parents expect of me." Josephine sighed quietly. "I can't say I hate them, but it's nice to take life at a slower pace with few concerns other than our daily work and spending time with my old and new friends. I feel a little selfish."

Raine shook her head. "Don't. We might like it here, but we're still contributing to the Magical Multitudes Project. Even if it feels like a vacation, it's not, and it's important to keep that in mind."

"Of course."

Silas nodded and for once, the quiet boy chose to make a rare comment. "I study during the summer. That's all I do. But this is nice. I miss studying sometimes, but I don't feel as nervous about stuff." He shrugged.

Milo grunted and nodded in approval, but he didn't say anything. One of the aspects of mazeball being canceled was the opportunity to get to know the more laconic and reserved Orono students.

William grinned, but his eyes remained closed. "I usually hang out with Cameron and his pack. You all work too hard, but this is nice too. It's so peaceful when mirror cats aren't trying to eat you and earthquakes aren't happening."

Everyone laughed.

Raine nibbled on her pineapple slice and glanced at Adrien. The elf sat and stared off at the horizon, a distant look in his eyes.

"Are you okay, Adrien? I know you spent some time doing sword practice, but I wasn't sure if being away from Guardian training for a couple of months and not in school bothered you."

He shook his head. "It did at first, but I can see the wisdom in not overtraining. I will admit I miss Christie far more than I anticipated, and that's made this troubling."

"Aww, that's so sweet," Evie said.

A few of the Orono boys grinned. Kelly, Dnai, and Heidi smiled and Josephine looked impressed.

His face reddened. "It's simply a statement of fact. Sweetness is irrelevant."

Sara shook her head. "If you're trying to sound less sweet, you're failing."

Adrien scoffed.

Finn snickered. "You really are like that guy from *Manic Human Dream Girl*, bro. Own it. It's not a bad thing to have a girl you care about."

The Light Elf continued to stare off into the distance. "I don't deny my feelings. I simply don't make a big deal of them."

"Okay, let's move away from Adrien's love life," Raine said. "He's not super-comfortable talking about it. I'm sorry for bringing anything up."

He waved a hand airily. "It's fine."

Finn smirked as he rested on his elbow. "What's he got to complain about? At least he has a girlfriend."

Asher sat up, his face illuminated by the soft glow of a nearby light orb. "It just struck me."

"That you don't have a girlfriend?"

He snorted. "No. I'm keenly aware of that, Finn." He sighed and shook his head. "This has nothing to do with that. Not directly. I thought about how we're all juniors—from both schools. Or we were. I mean technically, we're seniors now."

Philip yawned beside Sara. "Yeah, so what?"

"That means we have one last year." He held a single finger up. "They have all these magical academies, but it's not like they have magical colleges yet. Maybe there never will be. This whole chapter in our life is almost over."

Kelly wrapped her arms around her knees. "When you say it that way, it's almost depressing. I'll miss the OAAS. I feel like I became myself there. I didn't have a lot of friends back home because I could be nasty, and the school softened me up. You guys softened me up."

Raine nodded, curious about how much the girl had changed compared to some of her friends like William or Philip. "I feel the same way about the School of Necessary Magic. I liked my life before, but now, I feel like I am who I was always meant to be."

"I found a family there." William's expression softened and he looked at Cameron with gratitude. "A family who stood up for me against those who were supposed to be my family and turned their backs on me." He turned toward Evie. "And I found other people whom I can't live without. People I never expected to find."

Cameron frowned but it was thoughtful rather than anything negative. "I expected to take nothing but crap for four years for being a shifter, especially at a place with a reputation like the School of Necessary Magic. Some people might have had a few things to say to me, but outside my pack, I've never felt like I belonged. Now, I finally do, and that means more than I can say."

"Too bad they didn't start pro-Louper earlier." Finn stared at his hands. "I might have thought about giving that a try, but there aren't any amateur Louper leagues out there once you leave magic school."

Sara retrieved a single seed from her pouch. She tossed it a few yards away, and vines snaked out to form a small tangled mass on the beach. The other teens glanced from the vines to the kitsune.

She smiled. "When I started at the school, my magic hadn't come in and my family was ashamed of me. It was hard not to feel bad about myself because of that." A few tears seeped from the corner of her eyes. "But my friends stuck by me and encouraged me. Art Club inspired me to pursue my passion, and now, I have a future with my magic and my art that I never saw before."

Raine sighed softly. "Sometimes, you simply need to take a little time to stop and appreciate what you have. During the school semesters, there's also class, and with our luck, something weird always happens." She turned toward Josephine, the closest Orono student. "And from what you guys have told us, it isn't much different in Orono. Only a little more creature-centered."

A thoughtful look passed over the other witch's face. "I suppose if one wants a simple existence free of unusual encounters, attending a magic school is perhaps not the wisest way to go about it." She smiled. "You don't need to know magic to have a quiet office job."

Heidi looked like she wanted to say something before she simply smiled and shook her head.

Raine stretched a hand above her and peeked at the stars through her outstretched fingers. "Asher's right. The end's coming for all of us, and it'll be bittersweet. I know I'll be sad during graduation, but I also know this last year will be the best year yet because I have my friends and all my experiences behind me. Both of those have combined to turn me from the girl I was to the woman I'm becoming." She smiled at the Orono students. "And I have new friends. If you guys ever have a spare weekend, maybe you could come down— or we could try to work the opposite, but I doubt it. They like to keep us on a short leash at our school but given all the trouble we've landed in, maybe they aren't wrong to do that."

A slight grin appeared on Josephine's face. "I have to say that any school that ends up with a PDA agent investigating them for a year can't be boring. I always thought our school was a little too interesting, but yours makes ours sound mediocre."

Cameron snorted. "That PDA agent left at the end of the year, remember? Maybe we didn't make it clear."

"We don't have the PDA coming to our school." Josephine lay down again. "But I must admit I'm also disappointed that we're not interesting enough to have them come."

"Interesting?" Adrien asked. "That's one way to put it."

"When this is all over," Raine said, "we'll need to exchange contact information. Our school's fairly locked-down in terms of communication, but at least we'll have breaks when we can catch up. I feel like I've really gotten to know you guys, even though it's been weeks instead of years."

The other School of Necessary Magic students all nodded, smiles on their faces.

"That sounds great," Asher said cheerfully and the other Orono students agreed.

She sighed with real contentment. While she'd come for the learning experience and exposure to magical creatures, she would leave with eight new friends.

CHAPTER SEVENTEEN

Professor Powell marched along the beach and tapped his wand in his palm in time to his steps. A slight breeze blew off the ocean and brought the taste of the salt into Raine's mouth. The stars twinkled in the night sky above. As far as nature was concerned, it was merely another day, but to the students, it was so much more. The Fourth of July was a highlight on the calendar, even on a magical island.

"You all said you wanted to do this," the professor began, "and it's one of the few times we'll probably allow students to throw this kind of unrestrained and barely controlled magical power without concern. I assume, though, that it'd take a spectacular failure for you to somehow set the ocean on fire. Of course, you could accidentally hit the trees." He grinned. "But what's the Fourth of July without some fireworks?"

The gathered students all cheered. A few glanced at Adrien with questioning expressions on their faces.

"I'll pretend it's Bastille Day," the elf responded with a

smile. "Even I can appreciate a good explosion or two. Remember, I might be the stiff Guardian to all of you, but I do play Louper as much for fun as for the challenge."

Evie knelt in the sand where a ring of different-colored vials of potions rested on a small wooden tray in front of her. She'd worked feverishly over the last few days in her free time to prepare them with a little help from Professor Kaylis, who generously donated several ingredients from his own personal supply.

Professor Powell glanced down the beach and Raine followed his gaze. They were fifty yards away from the mazeball court. Even in a worst-case scenario, the piles of stone represented little risk to the students or their cabins.

Raine's heart almost danced with a new level of excitement. Even back home, there were severe limits on the type of conventional fireworks individuals could launch. Now, not only would she be able to generate a few explosions for entertainment value, she was encouraged to use her magic by one of her professors.

Friendship, relaxation, and searing the sky with ridiculous magic—they called it a summer research project, but she was convinced it was a vacation. The only thing that could make it better was if they stuck a small satellite library for the school on the island so she could at least read a book or two. Librarian Decker could probably find a solution, even with the magical interference.

Professors Hudson and Kaylis pored over some of the data collected that week, and Professor Tarelli had opted out of anything but hiding in her cabin. She'd told them firmly that loud noises and explosions set her on edge.

"Okay. Who will get us started?" Professor Powell

pointed into the heavens. "I'm not participating. I want this to be a strictly student-run activity. You've had days to prepare, so I hope you don't disappoint me or each other."

Sara stood and dusted the sand off her shorts. She took a few seeds from her pouch and nodded to William. He stood, his expression grim as if he were going into battle instead of starting a celebration.

"Ready?" she asked. "Thanks for agreeing to help Philip and me."

The half-Ifrit nodded. "No problem. I'm ready whenever you are."

With practiced ease, Sara arced the small seeds away from the group and up the beach and they burst into a tangled web of vines against the night sky. William raised his hands and gritted his teeth, his palm out. A jet of flame burst from his hand and he coated the vines with sweeping gestures. Soon, fire covered the plant lattice, a burning display that lit up the night.

Philip grinned and followed up with a rapid shower of silver sparks that rained over the burning tendrils.

The kitsune pointed at the web. "That's my take on those little snake fireworks. I used to love those as a kid."

Raine laughed. "I like it whenever there's a burn restriction, and they're all, 'Hey, you can still use snakes.' Boring, but yours is awesome."

"I live to serve." Sara bowed.

Adrien scrambled to his feet and raised his hands. "I have something both our countries can appreciate. We conveniently share the same flag colors." He shouted his incantations and blue, white, and red orbs hurtled upward, whistling as they ascended. Several seconds passed before they exploded with matching colors.

"Nice, Adrien," Asher said.

Everyone waited for a few seconds until the remnants of the display disappeared.

Raine sniffed at the air. "It's kind of strange to me, now that I think about it."

"Why is that?" Sara asked.

She pointed above them. "Our magic doesn't produce the kind of smells you get with normal fireworks."

Cameron wrinkled his nose. "Good. I hate those." He nodded meaningfully at her. "But stop stalling and let's see what you have, Raine. You wouldn't let even me see you practicing. So impress me and them with the power of the leader of the FBI Trouble Squad."

Raine laughed. "I might like investigating trouble, but Evie's better at magic than me. Still, I have a little something nice." She rose slowly, her wand pointed up, and murmured a complicated series of incantations while she made several precise movements with her wand. A glowing glyph appeared above her, then another. Days of practice and planning now came to fruition as the magic built in the air around her.

Professor Powell arched an eyebrow. "Maybe I should have had you all shield yourself before we began. I see some of you made plans to go above and beyond what I expected." He grinned. "Good."

Several more glyphs appeared above her until they surrounded her in a circle, and sweat rolled down the side of her face. She took several deep breaths in an effort to stabilize the complex flow of magic around her. If she'd attempted to pull this off during a confrontation, she would have lost control quickly, but the lower-pressure celebration suggested that she might be able to pull it off.

Several more seconds ticked by as the glyphs pulsed with power. She fed more magic into them until their light grew blinding.

A dozen white balls rocketed in rapid succession into the sky and traveled far higher than Adrien's earlier dual-nation patriotic display. They crackled and hissed rather than whistled.

Her first orb exploded in an expanding ring of white light. The next produced another ring, which overlapped and lingered for a few seconds. Soon, the sky above was filled with bright expanding rings.

The other students clapped.

"Nice one, Raine!" Cameron shouted.

Philip stuck his fingers in his mouth and whistled loudly.

Asher gave her a broad grin.

Raine took a few deep breaths and sank to her knees. "That took a lot out of me." She wiped the sweat off her brow. "I didn't think I could pull it off. In practice, I never managed to control that many of them before the spell collapsed."

Professor Powell gave her an approving nod. "An impressive combination of several things you've learned over the last several years. Maybe we should test students at the school by making them do fireworks displays." He winked. "You've set an impressive bar, and I'm interested to see what the other students bring."

"I think I'll go now," Evie said. She stood and nodded

before she pointed her wand at the tray and cast a lifting spell.

Everyone watched with eager expressions as the small tray floated up slowly, the potions still on it. Evie was the only one who had included any potions in her display.

"I hope I prepared the sequence right," she said. "The potion prep was the hard part, but I couldn't make extras to test this, so this might be really neat, or it might be lame."

Raine shook her head. "When it comes to potions, I have faith in you."

The Orono students exchanged glances before they focused on Evie again.

William raised his hand and grinned at her. "Just tell me when."

"I need it a little higher." She took a deep breath and continued to raise the tray. Ten feet. Twenty feet. Fifty feet. A hundred feet. She looked paler than normal. "Okay, do it, please."

The half-Ifrit nodded and launched a fireball. Everyone held their breath as the flame careened through the sky and enveloped the tray.

A massive boom followed, which elicited gasps of surprise. The sound rattled Raine's bones.

Spiraling fountains of flame lit the darkness, spun around each other, and left trails of glowing smoke in a myriad of colors. Crackling lines of energy twisted around the streams, something no conventional firework could ever hope to achieve.

Loud applause broke out on the beach, and Evie smiled happily at the display overhead. The fountains continued to pour their contents for a good half-minute before they finally subsided. The glowing smoke lingered and dimmed slowly.

"That's a good argument for learning potions," Finn said and clapped enthusiastically. "They should begin all freshmen potions sections with that kind of thing. Everyone would love the class then. I would have paid a lot more attention."

Evie sat once more and beamed with pride.

"We've seen interesting displays from my students, but how about a little effort from Orono?" Professor Powell asked.

After nodding to one another, Josephine, Heidi, and Kelly stood and pointed their wands at the same angle. They each began chanting a spell, their eyes half-closed in concentration. Evie's glowing smoke lingered in places, although it was far less bright than before.

Raine held her breath in anticipation. Everyone's efforts had been impressive in their own way, and she couldn't even imagine what the other girls might do. The seconds ticked by as they continued their complicated incantations.

The three Orono witches finished their spells. Three bright bolts of light launched into the heavens with a hiss. Everyone held their breath and waited for another massive explosion.

The first bolt fizzled. The second and third did the same thing.

The other students exchanged puzzled looks.

Raine sighed with real disappointment and looked furtively at the spellcasters. She didn't blame them or think them incapable. Complicated magic could fail, and at least they weren't hurt.

But there was no disappointment or concern on their faces, only anticipation. She returned her gaze to where the seemingly failed display had fizzled, her breath held yet again. Something was coming, but what?

The deep opening notes of Beethoven's Fifth Symphony thundered above them with bright flashes of light that matched the tempo. The next few notes followed, as if the sky was singing to the island.

"That's Jo for you," Asher said and shook his head with a broad grin. "She always has to class it up. I'm surprised Kelly was involved. It's not really her style."

"I heard that, Asher!" the witch shouted over the loud music. "Don't annoy me too much if you know what's good for you."

Raine barely noticed the exchange as she listened to the music and watched the vibrant display. She had spent years fixating on the utility of magic. From the very beginning, when they used stealth spells to sneak into the kemana, she'd allowed herself to think of magic as a tool, not a power.

As classical music played overhead, she took the time to appreciate that not everything she did with spells had to be about helping an investigation or apprehending chaos witches. Even the enchantments on her dresses during some of the dances were still more about treating her magic in a way that denied the pure fun it could be.

A broad smile settled on her face as wonder filled her heart. Magic was power. It was useful, but it was also fun.

The first full minute of the symphony played before the

music and pulsating lights died down. After Asher and Kelly's initial exchange, the others had listened in silence.

Everyone cheered at the completion of the spells. A few of the boys whistled in appreciation. The three Orono witches sat down. Heidi and Kelly both blushed, but Josephine looked serene, her chin raised and a soft smile on her face as if such complicated displays were something she did every day.

Asher cleared his throat. "Well, now you've set an even higher bar. That makes our school look good in front of the FBI Trouble Squad, but now, I have to prove myself. I have to outshine you but don't worry, I'm ready to put Evie's little potions display and that classical interlude to shame with the glorious display of magic that demonstrates the power of my line." He gestured widely. "I'm about to show you what centuries of Wood Elf tradition has brought forth. I'm about to—"

Raine's stomach clenched as a powerful pulse of magic passed over her.

A sudden massive tremor knocked Asher off his feet. He landed on his butt with a loud grunt. "Seriously? This has to happen *now?*"

The ground continued to shake, but with everyone on the beach and nowhere near any trees or buildings, no one was sure what they should do.

The Wood Elf muttered and shook his head.

Raine grabbed Cameron's hand, her stomach still tight from the violent tremors. She was sure she would have fallen too if she had been standing. It was definitely stronger than the last time.

Professor Powell frowned and pointed beyond the rock

wall. "Higher ground—now," he shouted. "There's a risk of a tsunami."

Raine blinked. They hadn't mentioned tsunamis before, but the earlier earthquakes had been weaker. She wasn't all that familiar with coastal earthquake protocol given where she lived normally during either the summer or the school year.

The students scrambled to their feet, a difficult task given the earth convulsing beneath them. Adrien, Asher, and Finn used burst spells to push them above the rock wall. Josephine remained close to Heidi and Kelly, her expression concerned. The other students reached the wall at the same moment that the ground stopped shaking.

The earthquake hadn't been long, but it had been intense. Raine breathed deeply and her gaze settled on Cameron, who frowned and looked a little angry—most likely because this was something over which he had no control. She made the decision right then and there to never live in California. Even if they didn't have earthquakes as often as New Firefly Island, she didn't think she could ever be comfortable in a place where the ground might become unstable at any moment.

Everyone regrouped near the cabins, walking slowly in case of aftershocks. The previous earthquakes had never had any, but no one could be sure given the apparent magical cause behind the tremors.

Professor Powell frowned and turned to study the ocean. "Even though the quake was strong, if it was that short, there's little risk of a tsunami. Still, we'll wait here on the higher ground for a while in case."

Finn smirked. "The island doesn't want to see any

magical fireworks from Asher, or maybe he was so desperate not to be shown up by Josephine that he caused the earthquake. Okay, bro, I get it. I'm impressed."

"Very funny." The Wood Elf rolled his eyes. "Maybe the island wanted to put me out of my misery before I had to see your lame effort. I saw you practicing the other day." He shook his head. "Seriously, it was sad."

"Says you." His friend shrugged.

Raine stared at the almost serene surface of the water. "It was definitely stronger, wasn't it? I didn't imagine that, did I?"

Professor Powell nodded grimly. "No, you didn't. It was definitely more powerful."

Her shoulders slumped. "If it gets much stronger, we won't be able to stay, will we? I obviously don't like them, but I also don't want to leave yet."

"We have to consider your safety," the professor said calmly. "I think the headmistress would have a few things to say to me if I came back with fewer students than I started with."

Concern passed over everyone's faces.

"But leaving is the last resort." The other three professors made their way toward the students and he paused to watch them approach. "And who knows, maybe we've simply had a run of bad luck."

She didn't need to be an FBI trainee to know he didn't believe that.

CHAPTER EIGHTEEN

Two days later, the idea of having to leave the island lingered in Raine's mind and wedged itself in her thoughts like a painful splinter. She had come to the conclusion that even though leaving would come eventually, the thought depressed her. Surprisingly, she'd adapted to the rhythms of her straightforward existence all too well.

"Are you okay, Raine?" Sara asked. "You look upset or something." She shrugged. "Not like you usually are."

She blinked a few times to refocus and nodded. "Sorry. I was a little lost in my thoughts. I didn't realize it was that obvious. I'm not trying to freak you out."

"Don't worry about freaking me out. If you want to talk, we can." The kitsune pointed to Professor Kaylis, who hummed to himself as he marched several yards ahead and pumped his wand like a baton in a marching band. "He's not exactly listening. It's like he's lost in his own world."

That day's team consisted of the professor, Raine, Sara, and Evie. They now traveled deep into the forest near the center of the island. An earlier trip had identified an inlet that allowed better access to the interior and this was their chosen route. The curious aspect was that it wasn't on any of the maps from earlier terrain surveys of the area. The professors theorized that it might have been created by the earthquakes.

Raine shrugged. "I'm not ready to go home." She laughed. "This basically teaches me that I really love camp, and I should have done a lot more of it when I was younger. I missed out on so much fun."

Her friends chuckled.

"It's nice, I'll admit." Sara looked around. "But I'm also getting to the point where I'm ready to go home, to be honest."

"Really?" she asked. "I thought you were having a good time, and you're spending so much time with Philip too."

"That's nice, but I think he would have preferred to do a charity project in a city. He doesn't complain too much, and he definitely enjoys more alone time with me, but he doesn't seem as contented as he usually is, and that makes me a little less happy." Sara shrugged. "But honestly, I miss my painting. There are so many inspirational things here, from the fireworks the other day to the animals and plants we run into. My mind is swimming with ideas. I've sketched things, but that's not the same as painting. I feel like my creativity is too bottled up, and it needs to be poured out sooner rather than later."

"I feel much the same." Evie patted her pocket. "I can do some potion work, but it's limited and more difficult here, and that baking experiment last week over the firepit?" She shuddered. "Well, like I said at the time, let's not talk about it again."

"I didn't realize people weren't having a good time." Raine chewed her lip and her glance flicked to the loudly humming Professor Kaylis, who now twirled his wand with surprising skill. "I feel bad now, like I didn't pay attention to your feelings."

Sara raised a hand in a placating manner. "It's not that I'm having a bad time. I'm still enjoying it here and the time I spend with my friends and Philip. It's simply that I feel what I don't have, too, and I feel it more each day. It's not really being homesick, but it's similar. Does that make sense?"

Evie nodded quickly. "Same here."

"Yes, that makes sense," Raine said. "I do miss reading case files. Maybe it's because I've overloaded on FBI stuff that I don't mind the vacation. I suppose I'll probably feel the same way as you guys do soon enough. This place is like an escape for me. A little refresher before we dive into that final year and face our future."

"We don't need to escape yet," Professor Kaylis said and halted abruptly. "I have the situation under control."

Raine looked at him and froze. The professor had stopped, his wand pointed forward and a concerned look on his face.

"Maybe you didn't understand what I meant, Professor," she explained. "I wasn't actually talking about today."

"It's fine, my girl." He adjusted his hat. "Everyone should raise shield spells just in case. I'm confident we can handle the threat, but I'd rather not have anyone hurt."

She didn't even bother to ask why and cast the spell

immediately, as did her friends. They looked around the area for the danger he had obviously seen.

Nothing seemed to stand out. Thick blankets of moss covered the tree trunks, but there weren't any strange vines or angry aquaboars, nor any mysterious shadows or mirror cats. There weren't even any glowing flowers. It looked like any other part of the forest and the background magic didn't feel any stronger.

Raine made another careful scrutiny of their surroundings, a little nonplussed by his behavior. "Professor, what's going on?"

Professor Kaylis nodded toward one of the trees. "Don't you see it?"

"I see moss." She frowned. "What am I supposed to see?"

"Look lower."

She lowered her gaze below the moss and noticed that numerous thin fibrous lines ran from the moss into the tree. "And what exactly am I looking at?"

"Don't blame the tree," the professor said quietly. "It's not the tree's fault. It's already dead, actually—a zombie tree, now. Very sad. Very sad, indeed."

"A zombie tree?" Raine shouted. "You have to be kidding me."

Birds took flight when the tree they stared at shook. Dirt blasted into the area accompanied by a volley of hollow pops. The tree somehow pulled its roots out of the ground and shimmering sparkles covered the moss.

"What the heck is that?" Sara pointed at the glittering growth with a half-disgusted, half-fascinated expression.

"A kind of magical parasite," Professor Kaylis explained. "It's interesting that even this kind of thing is on Earth now. They really can't survive without relatively high levels of magic. I wouldn't have thought there was enough, even here." The tree turned, its roots writhing below it, and swung a low-hanging branch at him.

The large white-haired man ducked with surprising agility before he raised his wand and shouted a cutting spell. White light flashed in front of his wand, and the offending branch dropped away from the tree, severed with a clean incision.

Several thick roots retaliated and slapped the professor to knock him backward.

Evie yelped as he catapulted several yards and disappeared into the underbrush.

Sara immediately threw several seeds. Her vines covered the infected tree, but its roots strained against the magical fibers and snapped them.

"Are we supposed to not hurt this thing?" Evie shouted. She raised her wand and managed to release a cutting spell and remove another branch. "He hurt it, didn't he?"

"He said it's dead already, so I think we can do what we need to do to protect ourselves." Raine pruned a few branches before she shrugged. "But how do you kill a zombie tree? It's not like it has a brain, to begin with."

The kitsune ducked as a branch swung at her and Evie severed it quickly. A moment later, a root smacked her and she screamed and crashed into another trunk. Her shield shimmered around her and her wand fell into a nearby bush.

She shook her head to clear it and plunged into the shrub to find her wand.

"Zombie trees." Raine removed two more branches in rapid succession. "That's so not fair."

A remaining branch managed to connect with Sara and the kitsune cartwheeled awkwardly with a yelp.

"Tell me about it," she shouted angrily.

Evie found her wand, raised it, and shouted another cutting spell.

Raine immediately followed-up with an attack of her own to remove the last major branch of the tree.

Several of the roots rose above the ground now, twitching and shuddering.

Sara's red hair popped out of the bushes several yards away, followed by her frowning face. "It has to be the moss. Burn it, Raine."

"I don't want to start a forest fire," she shouted to her friend.

Evie raised her wand. "You burn it, and I'll stand ready to put out any fires that spread."

Raine dodged a thrusting root and jogged a few yards back. She pointed her wand directly at the sparkling moss, took a deep breath, and spoke the incantation for a fireball.

A blast of flame roared away from her wand and rocketed into the verdant covering. Fire leapt from piece to piece and quickly consumed the growth on the surface bark. The roots slapped at random now and the tree shook violently. A few stray sparks scattered on either side and new fires were born.

Evie tossed her wand into her left hand and snatched two blue-tinted potions from her bag. She pulled the caps and hurled them to either side of the tree. With a hiss, frigid clouds smothered the fires and coated the nearby plants with a thin layer of frost.

The infected tree continued to shudder before it tilted ominously.

"Timber!" Raine yelled and rushed aside.

Evie and Sara fled in the opposite direction.

The thick trunk fell forward and stopped abruptly a few yards from the ground where it hung, suspended by nothing.

Professor Kaylis appeared from the brush with leaves and branches in his hair and his eyes narrowed. It was the closest to angry Raine had seen him during their entire time on the island.

His wand was pointed at the tree and he gritted his teeth. Slowly, he lowered his wand, and the trunk matched his movements before it settled harmlessly on the ground.

"That sort of reaction is why I try to not burn them," the professor said with a cheerful smile. "But all's well that ends well, I suppose." He marched toward the tree. "I had also hoped to take a sample of the moss for a few experiments, but self-defense is always more important. I'm glad I was able to see the famous FBI Trouble Squad in action." He crouched beside the scorched trunk and shook his head. "But what a waste of a perfectly good tree." He broke off some bark. "But maybe I can still achieve some research value from this sample."

Raine shook her head in disgust. "Zombie trees."

CHAPTER NINETEEN

A few days later, all the students marched through the forest behind Professor Powell. He had mentioned an important discovery from the previous day that he wanted to show them. Everyone had taken boats up the inlet and now, they were on a twenty-minute march through the forest, according to the professor, but he insisted that careful mapping had established a safe path. There should be no mirror cat ambushes or anything else dangerous.

"What's with the big mystery?" Sara asked with a frown. "Why can't you tell us what you want to show us?"

Philip nodded his agreement. "Yes, what's up?"

The professor glanced over his shoulder and offered her a mischievous smile. "Sometimes, a little anticipation isn't such a horrible thing. I would have thought your time on the island had made you more patient."

Sara rolled her eyes. "You're enjoying this way too much."

"Consider it a perk of being your instructor."

Adrien surveyed the area with his usual suspicion, but he didn't carry a sword. "You didn't need the other professors, but you needed all the students. That greatly narrows the range of possibilities." His fingers twitched for a moment.

"Does it?" the professor asked. "And what do you think that means? What do you think is going on?" He turned to Raine. "Your thoughts?"

She kept her wand in hand, ready for whatever mirror cat or zombie tree might dare to attack them. "I think you want to train us. I think there's some sort of threat in the center of the island that is dangerous enough to require more than a few students, but not so deadly as to require all the other professors. You like things more hands-on, and you're the one who teaches us how to protect ourselves. It makes sense that you would want us to get some practical experience."

"That's an interesting theory." He grinned. "It might even have the virtue of being true. Or maybe not."

Cameron scoffed and plodded on in front of Raine. "Sara's right. You are enjoying this too much."

Dnai walked with the rest of the students. The density of trees and branches on this part of the island made flying pointless except for tiny birds.

"It might be some cool plants," she said with a shrug. "Something that we'll all find interesting."

Professor Powell continued to smile as he pushed past a few trees and stepped over several logs snapped in different places. He gestured to the fallen trees. "They were so close together, they almost worked as a fence and so we hadn't explored this area yet. We intended to come in from a different angle in a few days. The earthquakes probably felled them, given how recently they appear to have fallen."

Raine's eyes widened as the students stepped beyond the logs and past another wall of thick bushes. A huge pond—almost a small lake—lay beyond the shrubby growth. A few bright orange ducks floated on top. They caught sight of the two-legged threats and immediately took flight.

Professor Powell gestured to the pond as the other students caught up. "This is, to the best of our knowledge, the only decent-sized body of fresh water on the island. The initial surveys missed it, or perhaps the earthquakes changed the local topography enough to generate the pond. I know it has to be annoying to be on an island in summer and not able to swim, but there is still the risk of too many things that can eat you with one bite in the ocean. When we found this, I thought it might be a nice little reward for all your hard work so far." He grinned. "See. Sometimes, it is worth waiting for the surprise."

"Nice, Professor. Very nice." Asher chuckled. "So that's why you taught us that drying spell the other day."

"Exactly." He raised his wand. "And this gives me a good opportunity to teach you another spell that might prove a little useful during your stay on the island."

"What's that?" Adrien asked. He walked closer to the water.

It was mostly clear, although caches of leaves floated on the top, along with a few bugs. Raine would have preferred water without insect life or debris, but she also didn't want to pass up the chance to swim, especially given how muggy the air was that day. Her shorts and shirt stuck to her sweaty body.

Professor Powell circled his head with a finger. "It's an air bubble spell. It's a nice way to temporarily breathe in water without the complexities of filtering, transfiguration, or other such methods." He stepped toward the edge of the pond. "The major disadvantage of the spell I'm about to teach is that it's far more limited than other magical methods you might use to breathe underwater. The simplicity makes it attractive, though."

"How is it limited?" Raine asked.

The students now stood near the pond with varying mixtures of excitement and curiosity on their faces as they glanced from the water to the professor.

"The magic is exactly what it sounds like," he explained. "It's an air bubble, not a pressure bubble. This isn't the kind of spell you want to use for deep-sea diving. It's simply something suitable if you want to, say, hang out at the bottom of a pond for a few minutes without holding your breath. The disadvantage is that it has to be refreshed fairly regularly, and the movements necessary can't be performed correctly in water, even if you can speak the incantations normally into the air bubble. That means you need to have careful timing and ensure that you have enough air."

Cameron kicked at the edge of the water. "Can you cast it on someone else?"

"Yes." Professor Powell nodded. "Definitely."

Evie knelt and trailed her hand through the water. "It sounds good enough for a little fun. We're not responsible for fish during the survey, so it's not like we need a spell that lasts super-long."

"Exactly." Professor Powell smiled and raised his wand. "The key, really, is to size it right and fit it to your head. It's not all that different from some of the other spells that create bubbles." He twisted his wand. "The motions are similar, as are the incantations and the general level of magic required. It's simply that this one sucks in air while it's created." He gestured for Cameron to come closer. "Since you don't need to learn the spell, how about I demonstrate on you? That is if you don't mind."

The boy stepped closer and shrugged. "Fine. How much air does this have, though? I'm fairly good at holding my breath. If it's less than a few minutes, there's not much point."

"Properly performed, it will generally be about ten to fifteen minutes of air." He pointed his wand at Cameron. "The thing is, if you try to size it too big, it collapses. If it's too small, it can't hold much air. It's a careful balance."

The students nodded.

The professor made a few quick movements with his wand with an emphasis on twists. He uttered the incantation slowly and stressed the pitch emphasis changes necessary in each syllable before he repeated it more quickly. A blue bubble appeared around Cameron's head.

The shifter opened his mouth and spoke, but the sound was too muffled to hear.

"Yet another disadvantage for the basic air sphere," Professor Powell said. "You can hear decently enough with it over your head, but it's hard for anyone else to understand you."

Cameron shrugged. He knelt on the ground and stuck his head in the water.

Everyone leaned closer to watch him. He stuck his thumb up and held his head under the surface.

The professor nodded at him. "Strictly speaking, I could leave out some parts of the incantation so you don't have the visible blue bubble, but it acts as a kind of status report. The whiter it becomes, the less air you have left. I wouldn't trust in timing when it comes to breathing."

The shifter remained where he was and the bubble around him stayed blue for a long moment. Finally, he raised his head.

Professor Powell touched his wand to the magic sphere, spoke an incantation, and it vanished. Cameron's head remained dry.

"How did that feel?" the professor asked.

"Like I was breathing normally," the student said with a shrug. "It's like having a helmet on that doesn't weigh anything."

Asher glanced at the water. "And you didn't feel any pressure or anything?"

He shook his head. "Nothing like that."

Professor Powell shook his wand enthusiastically. "Now, let me see you practice, and I'll leave you to have a little fun for a while."

CHAPTER TWENTY

No one had any swimsuits on them and they didn't have their backpacks either. Not only had they not thought about that when they set out, but the professors from both schools had also explicitly told them not to pack swimsuits as they didn't want to encourage anyone to attempt any real swimming in the ocean around the island.

Fortunately, the lack of these wasn't much of a concern thanks to the drying spell they'd learned. The students eagerly removed their boots, socks, and belts and emptied their pockets before diving into the water.

Silas and Finn demurred, neither eager to get wet even with the magical drying potential, but everyone else enjoyed the cool interlude.

Raine hadn't swum in a pond in a long time, and she remembered the last experience as frigid and unpleasant. The water in the New Firefly Island pond was surprisingly warm—much warmer than she would have thought given the relatively cool temperatures at night. Some hot springs were involved, she was sure of it.

She drifted around in the water and savored the sensation for several minutes, occasionally smiling at Cameron or one of her friends or splashing them playfully.

Sara emerged from below the surface, a blue bubble around her head. She canceled the spell and splashed a little water on Philip. "Since the professor taught us the spell, we might as well really use it. It's almost like he told us to—dared us to, even."

The kitsune might have been scared off pranks because of the chaos-related incidents during the last prank war, but she still possessed a competitive and confrontational streak.

Philip frowned. "Meaning what exactly?"

"Let's have a little competition." She grinned. "When I swam around, I saw some tunnels down there. We should have a contest to see who can go the farthest on one casting of the spell."

"That doesn't sound too bad." The wizard nodded, his eyes bright with anticipation.

Raine smiled. "It sounds fun."

Milo shrugged. "I'm fine hanging around up here."

Josephine kept her eyes closed as she floated on her back. "As am I. Honestly, I'm so completely relaxed, I don't see the point of trading that for a competition."

Heidi nodded in agreement.

Dnai made a face. "I don't like the sound of underwater tunnels. It sounds like something that will scratch my wings."

Evie shrugged. "I'm enjoying just swimming around. Sorry."

Raine wasn't surprised. Her friend wasn't much interested in any competition that didn't have to do with baking.

"I'll stay where Evie is," William said. He frowned. "And I don't much like going underwater."

Raine wondered if that was related to his Ifrit nature but decided to let it be. He might be uncomfortable about it or even slightly afraid, and calling him out in front of all the Orono students would be rude.

Kelly pointed a thumb at her chest. "I'm in, Raine. I need something to satisfy my competitive urges since I lost mazeball. It has to come out somehow."

Asher nodded. "I'm in, too."

"I'll go where you go, Raine." Cameron smiled and seemed to actually enjoy the challenge.

Adrien shook his head. "I'd prefer to stay on the surface for now."

"Okay." Sara looked around. "Me, Raine, Cameron, Kelly, Philip, and Asher, then? Does that sound about right?"

The competitors all nodded.

The kitsune grinned. "Everyone should get their spells ready. This is one time where I love not having to use a wand. It makes it easier to swim."

Raine headed over to the shore to grab her wand. She created an air bubble over Cameron's head and then her own before she summoned a light orb for each of them. Everyone else prepared their own magic.

"Let's go!" Sara shouted and turned to dive deeper into the water.

Raine sank beneath the water, not in a particular hurry.

It wasn't a speed race, and a few seconds here or there wouldn't make much difference.

The water surrounding her was from a pond, not a pool, and that nature was reflected by the small but otherwise normal fish that darted around several feet down. A few had brushed her legs earlier.

Twigs and rocks covered the bottom, and enough dirt was suspended in the water to reduce visibility. The light orb helped but not as much as she would have liked.

She dove deeper and the lights of the others glowed near her. The dark holes that marked the tunnels all lay near the base and presented three different paths. She waited for Cameron to go through one before she took a different route. Sometimes, it was good to not allow him to be overprotective and remind him that she was capable of taking care of herself.

Raine swam for a couple of minutes and kept a wary eye on the color of her bubble. She could hold her breath for a couple more minutes if it became necessary, but she didn't want to push her luck. Her feet kicked and propelled her deeper into the tunnel.

A few fish swam past but nothing intimidating or dangerous-looking.

Dnai had been right. The narrow tunnels would have made it difficult for her to navigate. It occurred to her that the girl might previously have had trouble in a similar situation.

She glanced behind her and realized she'd been the only one to choose her tunnel. Perhaps she should return. They hadn't really specified any real winning conditions, but she was motivated more by curiosity to keep going than any concern over winning their diving competition.

A few more minutes passed, and the blue had noticeably faded from her breathing sphere. She was about to turn when she noticed a faint glow ahead and couldn't resist moving forward. Perhaps it was some sort of fish trick, which might prove interesting.

Another minute of swimming brought her to a cavern filled with a soft green light above the water. She surfaced, canceled her spell, and took a deep breath.

"Huh. Interesting."

Glowing rocks covered the walls of the surprisingly vast cavern and provided the illumination that had lured her there. Two small tunnels led out in addition to the one through the water, and both looked large enough for a person to fit through. Thick clusters of stalactites hung from the ceiling. Water dripped steadily from several of them, and the stalagmites on the ground suggested that they had been there for a long time.

Raine caught movement from the corner of her eye and she spun that way, her wand up. A small glowing jellyfish-like creature floated through the air toward one of the tunnels and a quiet buzz accompanied its flight.

"Huh. That's cool." She smiled and turned to point it out to Cameron before she remembered that he wasn't in the cavern with her and sighed. "That's right."

She took a few splashing steps until she was completely out of the water. Her soaked clothes dripped around her feet. She looked from one tunnel to the other and curiosity poked in the corner of her mind. One foot followed another, and she stopped and looked around before she reached the exits.

It wasn't FBI training that stopped her but experience on her many semester adventures. She felt like she was being watched.

"Asher? Cameron? Sara? Kelly? Philip?" she shouted. Her voice echoed in the cavern but no one replied.

Raine cast a shield spell and frowned. "Is anyone there?"

Again, there was no response.

She stared at the tunnels and shook her head. "I've watched enough horror movies not to wander into weird tunnels by myself," she muttered. She sighed and shook her head before she cast a new air bubble.

The additional tunnels would have to wait. For all she knew, there could be mirror cats in there—or something worse. With her luck, there was probably a floating zombie jellyfish waiting to try to eat her in the darkness.

She waded back into the water and pondered the anatomical features of a zombie jellyfish.

A few minutes later, she emerged in the main pond. All her other friends were on the surface, including a worried-looking Cameron.

"I was about to go looking for you," he growled and his eyes flashed yellow. "You took way longer than anyone, and I thought…" He sighed. "Well, we didn't know what happened. What took you so long? Did your spell last the whole time?"

Raine nodded toward the water. "The underwater

tunnels open into a cavern. I recast the spell there. Plus, there were some other tunnels, too, and weird gleaming rock and a floating jellyfish that glowed. Except that was in the air." She shrugged. "It was interesting and I wanted to explore more, but I felt a weird vibe so I came back."

"Smart move," he said. "You should always trust your instincts. They haven't failed you yet, even all the way to knowing something was up with Madelyn."

Asher scooped some water in his palm. "Oh, it was probably only a hungry water dragon you woke up. He's there to show you that not all dragons are like Dorvu. He needs blood and flesh!"

She laughed. "I'd be impressed if a fully-grown dragon could fit down there."

"It's probably best to leave it alone for now," Adrien called. "If there are weird creatures inside, you don't know how dangerous they might be."

Raine nodded. "Fair enough. It's not like the cavern is going anywhere."

Sara floated toward them. "You found a whole new cavern and worried us. I guess that means you win the contest." She splashed water in her face. "Now, let's see if you can win the water war."

Finn frowned from the shore on the opposite bank. He stared intently at the ground. "We should get going."

"Why?" Cameron asked, his brow furrowed in concern.

The wizard squatted and pointed to the mud at the shore. "Because there are footprints here that don't belong to us."

"It's probably from Professor Powell or the others," Raine said.

Finn shook his head. "None of us walked around on this side."

Adrien swam toward him. "You said you had a weird vibe, Raine. Maybe there was someone else in that cavern. Finn's right. We should go."

CHAPTER TWENTY-ONE

Professor Powell and Professor Hudson both frowned as Raine finished her explanation while seated at one of the camp tables. The other students added a few other details, including Finn. Even Professor Kaylis looked worried, but Professor Tarelli appeared to be excited.

The huge smile on her face could easily have made someone think it was her birthday.

The Nygan professor bounced a few times. "Don't you realize what you've found? Do you have any inkling at all?"

"I think we found trouble," Raine said crisply. "I honestly don't know, Professor. That's why we're telling you." She glanced at the two professors from her school. "I've learned to not keep information from the experienced magicals who might be able to help me."

Professor Tarelli shook her head. "No, no. You don't understand. Those weren't jellyfish you saw, and they aren't trouble."

"Huh? Sure. I understand that they floated in the air

and aren't normal jellyfish. Wait. Why do you even care about those?"

The professor sighed. "You still don't understand. It's what those creatures represent. They are a kind of commensal magical creature that is normally associated with much larger creatures—almost exclusively so. It's a particularly special find, especially because of the implications for what else we might find in the area." She rubbed her hands together with obvious enthusiasm. "Their presence here suggests there's something around that is considerably more impressive than skimmers. There might even be a Kraken." She scratched her cheek and squinted. "Or even something much larger. No, no. That's impossible. We'd know. It obviously has to be sea-based, though. I think we would have detected signs of anything that large that lived or nested on the land as we've at least sampled most major regions of the island. Hmm. So many possibilities. Oh, how wonderful. You have such good luck."

Raine winced. "Wait. A Kraken? Now I'm really glad we didn't try to swim in the ocean."

Several other students grimaced.

"Yes! Wouldn't that be wonderful? There shouldn't be enough magic for that kind of creature to currently survive on Earth, but this might be a special case." Professor Tarelli sighed with contentment. "Good job, Megan. You have a good nose for finding unusual things. I see why they like your CIA Berserker Brigade."

She didn't even bother to correct the professor about her or the squad's name. Instead, she sighed and shook her head.

A Kraken? She had thought the mirror cats and zombie

trees were bad enough, but now her wonderful vacation island might have a Kraken prowling the seas around it. All her hard-earned relaxation had vanished.

Her breath caught. She was missing something else much more important. Her heart thundered with a new impetus that might be anticipation. There were different ways to enjoy the island. She'd let the lazy pace focus her on one way and ignored the obvious.

Professor Powell held a hand up. "I'm far less concerned about any theoretical Kraken than the footprints the students found—and the fact that Raine felt like she was being watched in that cavern. That has implications, and they don't involve large sea monsters. The students can deal with animals and even magical animals, but people are more complicated, especially if they are who I think they are."

"What do you think?" Raine asked. "Another survey group? Maybe they simply forget to tell you or they're eco-tourists."

Professor Kaylis sighed and shook his head. "No. It was made very clear to me that we would be the only ones on the island. If it were another survey group, they would use the cabins and the dock, not go in and out of ponds in the center of the island. Besides that, travel to this island is restricted. Because of the magical interference, they couldn't have portaled in easily. Unfortunately, I've been worried about another possibility, and the evidence suggests my concerns were well-founded. Alas. Things are about to get complicated."

Raine frowned and fixed him with a challenging look. "What concerns, Professor?"

"This is an island filled with rare magical animals, especially if you're talking about limiting your supply to Earth. Some of the creatures here may very well not exist anywhere else on Earth, and it would be difficult to import them from Oriceran without considerable trouble." Professor Kaylis paced as he spoke, his demeanor tense and serious. "Whenever you limit the supply of animals, one deadly and unfortunate possibility always arises. It's simple supply and demand."

Adrien narrowed his eyes. "You're talking about poachers, aren't you?"

"Exactly, my boy. Poachers." He stopped pacing and nodded toward the forest. "Many of these species are extremely valuable on the black market, either whole or for their individual parts. If there are poachers seeking magical animals, they will be very dangerous men who understand both the risks of the animals and the risks of getting caught, especially by certain Oricerans who take an even dimmer view of that sort of activity than many Earth groups and governments." He looked at the other professors. "I recommend that the students only go out with a professor until we can firmly establish what's going on. It's too much of a risk otherwise. Such men are dangerous. I've dealt with them before."

"Agreed," Professor Powell said. "We'll need to establish if there are poachers, and if so, we might need to contact the government so they can handle it."

Professor Hudson nodded her agreement. Professor Tarelli mumbled something about Kraken habitat ranges and didn't seem to be aware of the other conversation.

"I'm sorry." Professor Powell smiled apologetically at

the students. "You lost your mazeball and now, you've lost your pond."

"Do we have to leave?" Raine asked, her tone even. "I'd hate to take off early."

"Possibly. The earthquakes are unpredictable, but at least we know they won't attack someone out of greed. We'll have to see what happens." He shrugged. "But we can't make any promises either way."

She nodded and tried to keep the smile on her face. Her heart pounded and her palms were sweaty. It was a genuine mystery. She had enjoyed her time on the island, but her old instincts now kicked in and demanded that the mystery be solved and the criminals caught. While she wouldn't go against the professors, she could help them when they went out.

There was no reason to leave and have the government solve everything. Four trained magical instructors and fifteen students would be more than enough to stop a few poachers.

Professor Kaylis cleared his throat. "Is that clear to everyone? For now, we'll need you to stick close to camp unless you're with a professor. I know it's an inconvenience, and I hope I'm wrong, but I won't disrespect you by pretending that poachers aren't a serious concern. I can't stress how dangerous these kinds of men can be."

The students all nodded, their faces etched with concern. Raine did her best not to grin.

Cameron eyed her, suspicion in his eyes. He leaned over to whisper in her ear. "Don't get too excited. We won't run off and do anything without the professors."

She nodded quickly. "I know."

CHAPTER TWENTY-TWO

Xander sighed and shook his head as he studied the shoreline. The students' footprints were there, but there was no sign of any others. He sucked in a breath and exhaled slowly.

Eleanor stared at the mud and scowled uneasily. "Do you think they misinterpreted what they saw? Mistook one of their own footprints?"

"No, I don't. They might be overeager, but they're not fools." He narrowed his eyes. "I think that whoever they almost bumped into was smart enough not to attack a large group of students and also to try to cover their tracks in case said students alerted their professors." He squatted for a closer look. "And in my experience, people only cover their tracks when they have something to hide." He barked out a sudden laugh. "I would know."

She looked at him like he'd lost his mind. He could understand her reaction. Even though she'd always been respectful of him despite his past, she could never really understand on the same level that Mara did.

"You're wondering why I'm laughing?" Xander asked.

"The thought did cross my mind, yes. This doesn't strike me as an even sardonically amusing situation, but I'm open to having my mind changed."

He stood and smiled. "It was simply that I tried to decide who has the bad luck in this situation."

"Bad luck?" Eleanor glanced into the water. "What do you mean?"

"Everywhere those kids go, trouble follows them, even when they don't actively look for it." He turned slowly in search of anything unusual or odd magical sensations. There wasn't anything beyond the normal high background magic of the island. "It's been like that from the beginning. At least with Alison and Izzie, the trouble involving them made sense given who Izzie truly was. But with these kids, it's like the universe is determined to prove something to us. Or at least that's one possibility, but they're not the only ones who get themselves in trouble."

"And what's the other? Are you talking about the OAAS students?"

"No. Not them at all, but that's a third possibility." His jaw tightened. "I meant someone else from the School of Necessary Magic. There's only one professor who was poisoned in the last few years when leaving campus. If there is such a thing as bad luck, maybe I'm as much as a cause as they are. I find trouble exactly like they do."

Eleanor scoffed. "You can't honestly believe that, Xander."

"I can't say that I do, but I also have a hard time totally not believing it." Xander crouched at the water's edge and his boots sank into the soft mud. "We still don't know who poisoned me. I know it doesn't have anything to do with poachers who might be on the island, but I can't say I don't think about it often, especially because Mara made serious sacrifices to save me. Until we get to the bottom of that, there's a threat. I don't care much about the possible danger to me, but I don't want those kids dragged into something that has nothing to do with them."

"Why would they get dragged into something like that?" She looked confused. "Whoever poisoned you didn't target any of the students."

He stood and pointed his wand at an untouched patch of mud and cast a revelation spell. The thin outline of a boot appeared. "Ah, here we go. They were smart enough to literally cover their tracks but still not thorough enough to think about us coming in with our own magic."

"You didn't answer my question." She folded her arms over her chest. "What does danger to you have to do with Raine and her friends?"

"Did you see Raine when we were talking?" He shook his head and sighed.

"What about her?"

"She tried to hide it, but she was excited. I'm certain of it."

Eleanor nodded. "We've inculcated a certain attitude among all the students—a certain independence—and she and her friends have taken that to another level, but isn't that a good thing? She'll train for the FBI soon. They aren't the same children who started school three years ago. They've proven themselves. I'm not saying we throw them to the lions, but we also can extend them some trust."

"Not the same kids?" Xander snorted. "They damned

well are. Yes, they aren't young children, but they are still children. I'm proud of how well they have handled themselves, but I also know that if dark wizards show up to kill me, those kids could suffer, exactly like when the dark wizards showed up last time." He frowned. "If only I'd known the truth, maybe I could have done something."

"You don't know that. None of us know that. The only people to blame for those incidents are the dark wizards behind them." She stared at him, her gaze evaluating him before she nodded. "And that's who you think poisoned you? Dark wizards?"

"It makes the most sense. They're probably afraid to attack the school directly because they know we're too fortified now." He cast another revelation spell and found a different boot print. "I'm not saying they plan to attack the school. I'm saying this is probably something personal from my past, and I don't want any student to suffer because of it. I'll handle my own mess and problems. No more sacrifices on my behalf."

"And what do you plan to do, then? I can't believe you'll leave the school. I don't say this for your sake, but I do honestly believe you're an asset to the school. Mara certainly does."

He allowed himself a smirk and a quick laugh. "I've finally earned Mara back after losing her. If I leave now, I might lose her again. No, I can't leave, but it also means that when I get back to school, there has to be some way I can look into this or draw out whoever was responsible."

"But what and how?" Eleanor cast her own revelation spell in another patch of mud. She found no boot- or footprints, only reptile and amphibian tracks. "It's not exactly like you or Mara ignored the issue when it arose the first time. Other than potentially tracking it to external food, you hit a dead end, and it's been a couple of years now. It's not like new evidence will spontaneously appear."

"I can't believe someone would go through all the trouble to use such a powerful magical poison and then simply give up." He spun toward a nearby tree, his wand at the ready, only to find a few confused birds who promptly squawked and flew away.

"Far be it for me to suggest this, given everything that's happened over the last seven or so years," she said tentatively, "but is it possible that you're too paranoid? It might have been a crime of opportunity that won't be repeated."

"There's no such thing as too paranoid." He shook his head. "Believing that is the only reason I'm still alive. It's not like that poisoning was the first time someone tried to eliminate me. It's merely the most recent attempt and the closest anyone's gotten in a while."

"Understood, but as I see it, you have a limited number of choices."

"I know. But it's something I think I'll need to resolve sooner rather than later."

Eleanor nodded toward the water. "I understand, but now, we should focus."

He nodded. "Fair enough."

"Should we examine the cave?"

Xander pointed his wand at his head. "Yes."

"I overheard them talking," Raine murmured to the rest of the Trouble Squad. They were clustered around one of the tables near the firepit, waiting for the day's classic camp meal of baked beans and potatoes.

Adrien slid a furtive glance at Professor Kaylis' cabin. All four professors were sequestered inside to discuss things. They'd moved indoors when they'd seen Raine lurking around them.

"What did you hear?" Adrien asked. "I mean exactly, not what you think."

"They definitely found more evidence of someone in that cavern and even went farther than I did before turning back. In fact, they found evidence of multiple people." She nodded, satisfied with the progress of the case.

Sara frowned. "So there really are poachers here?"

"Probably." She shrugged.

Philip frowned. "That's so uncool. Jerks."

Asher wandered over to their table, a slight smile on his face. "Oh, I know that look, mainly because I have it a lot. You have trouble in mind, don't you?"

Raine shook her head. "We're only talking about the poachers."

His face darkened. "I might not be a Wood Elf on Oriceran, but I'm still a Wood Elf, and it's hard to be one and not want to bash in a poacher's face." He dropped onto the bench beside Raine. "They had to screw our trip up, and they're messing with the animals. There's nothing worse than a poacher. They're the definition of takers."

"Unless they aren't poachers," she pointed out. "We haven't found any dead animals, right? Wouldn't we have?"

"The point of poaching in this situation is to take the

animals with you. You won't only take a tooth or horn or something from these animals." He shrugged. "Besides, who else do you think they might be?"

"I don't know." Her gaze flicked to Adrien.

"It's not the Raven Clan." The Light Elf shook his head. "Not here and not like this. They wouldn't be this subtle, especially with us isolated on an island in limited numbers."

"I suppose you're right. The simplest explanation is usually the best." Raine blew out a breath. "We'll probably find out soon enough. Until then, there's not much we can do."

Cameron eyed her, his disbelief etched into his face. "And you're okay with that?"

"Okay with waiting until additional evidence is available for the case?" She smiled. "The evidence drives the case. That's the FBI way."

CHAPTER TWENTY-THREE

Professor Hudson strolled through the forest, her wand held loosely in her hand. Raine, Philip, Sara, and Asher walked behind her. The professor had barely said ten words in as many minutes.

Raine's gaze darted to every single new shadow or shifting bush as if a gang of thugs might ambush them at any moment. Even though it had been several days since their trip to the pond, she was surprised the professor now took them to survey an area near the center of the island. While they weren't too close to the pool by her estimation, she'd assumed the professors intended to keep the students well clear of the area.

There was also the issue that they traveled through mirror cat territory, but she assumed the professor was confident in her ability to handle the predator without harming it.

She nodded confidently. The assumption made sense. Technically, they had disabled the cats without hurting them, so there was no reason to expect that the more experienced witch would have any difficulty.

A tense silence clung to the group, which highlighted the whistle of the wind and chirp and rustle of nearby animals. She was possibly the only one more worried about two-legged than four-legged predators.

Asher cleared his throat. "Geeze, I can't take this anymore. It's killing me."

Professor Hudson glanced over her shoulder. "Take what?"

"Everyone is so quiet like we're ninjas or snipers or something." He shrugged. "It's not like we're trying to sneak around, so why not talk? It makes me tense to walk along and not say anything.

"Feel free to speak on whatever topic you choose. I apologize for my current lack of pedagogical effort." A faint smile appeared on the woman's face. "That's mostly because we've already surveyed most of this area. I'll be more than willing to expand on subjects of interest when we arrive in the new survey area. I've tried to focus and pay attention to any species in this area not previously recorded in case, though."

Sara shrugged. "I was quiet because I was looking for poachers or poacher tracks."

Raine chuckled nervously. "Me, too."

"I don't want to think about them." Asher sighed. "Maybe they got scared and left. I hope so. I'd be happier if they left before they hurt any of the other rare animals around here."

The professor turned to stroll between two large tree trunks and over a glowing toadstool. "That's not an impossibility. If the footprints found at the pond were in fact from poachers, the fact that they tried to conceal them does indicate that they are concerned about being caught, which suggests a certain limitation on their range of ability and even their arrogance. They obviously don't believe they are free to act with impunity. They also might not be sure about who is present on the island. That would be an optimal scenario, but we also can't be sure it was poachers. That's merely Professor Kaylis' theory. There are other possibilities."

"Whoever it is, they aren't supposed to be here," Raine said. "That means they're probably a dangerous criminal."

"While they might not be dangerous criminals, it is true that travel to this island is currently largely prohibited so that does raise concerns about who would ignore such restrictions. Caution remains warranted at the very least." She stopped and raised her wand and her nostrils flared. "Everyone, be very quiet," she whispered, "and prepare a shield spell."

The students cast the spell as she crept forward. After a few steps, Raine noticed the cause of her concern—a large mirror cat sprawled on the ground. There were no shadows or other creatures in sight, but there were more than enough trees and bushes to hide behind.

Professor Hudson's frown turned into a look of disgust. She lowered her wand and shook her head. "Oh, no."

Raine frowned and peered at the sleeping cat. She took a few steps closer. The slight change in angle revealed darkened and scorched flesh on the side. The feline wasn't breathing, and its eyes were open.

Asher jogged forward, his face tight and angry. He drew

closer to the animal and his expression darkened with each step.

"It's too late." Professor Hudson shook her head. "She's already dead."

"I'm not an expert on magical forensics, but I've read through enough books and files from Agent Connor to recognize a few things." Raine approached the body and pointed at the burn. "That wound isn't from a grenade. I guarantee that. It's certainly not from a gun. It could be from a flare, but there's an obvious blast pattern."

The Wood Elf glared at the corpse. "Come on. We've seen this kind of thing before even if we've not seen it on a wild cat. This is obviously from a fireball."

The professor nodded grimly. She raised her wand and whispered an incantation. The wound glowed lightly. "Magical residue, and fairly recent. Probably from today judging by the glow."

"That's consistent with the state of the victim's body," Raine declared and shifted completely into FBI trainee mode. "I'm not one hundred percent sure of non-human decomposition, but this body looks very fresh. Like today fresh, which is in line with what you said, Professor."

Asher slammed his fist into his palm. "So they're not even trying to sell them? They're simply killing them? Is that what this is—some guys sneaking onto this island to kill rare animals? It's not like them selling them would have made it all better, but this—" He growled and spat in disgust.

"We need to regroup at the camp and figure out how to best handle this." Professor Hudson frowned and pointed her wand skyward. A bright blue flare rocketed from the tip of her wand.

Raine tore her attention away from the flare to look at the slain creature. They'd tried so hard not to hurt any of the animals only for someone else to come and kill them. As far as she was concerned, the mirror cat was a murder victim, and she wanted to bring her killers to justice.

Professor Tarelli shook her head, a sad look in her eyes. "It's definitely poachers. Basil was right. I suppose the animals are fortunate in that these criminals chose to come at a time when a reasonable number of people are exploring the island."

The small group had returned to the camp immediately after their discovery. Now, the students sat spread between the tables while the professors stood near them.

Adrien frowned. "If it's poachers, why did they kill the animal and leave the body? Where's the money in that? Isn't that the point? If they're hunters, why wouldn't they take a trophy? It doesn't make any sense."

Asher nodded. "They could simply be sick freaks."

Professor Tarelli sighed. "No. I'm more convinced than ever that this is about breeding. A dead female mirror cat at this time of year is telling evidence. The males are the ones that tend to patrol the territory. The mothers stay near their dens to feed and protect the young."

Raine frowned. "Wait. So there are kittens out there?"

The professor gestured toward the forest. "There are,

but my guess is that the poachers killed the mother to take the kittens. It's difficult to control fully grown mirror cats, but if you acquire them as kittens, it's possible. It's something breeders do, and I've heard of this kind of thing before on Oriceran."

The Wood Elf bolted out of his seat. "So they killed the mom, and they're running off with the kittens? We have to find them before they get away."

"What a pointless waste." Professor Kaylis sighed with heavy regret.

Professor Hudson frowned. "I'll need to contact Fish and Wildlife. They have primary anti-poaching jurisdiction, even if the animals are unusual."

Asher shook his head. "But you'll have to go all the way to the mainland, then contact them, and even if they decide to do something, it'll take them forever to get here. By then, the poachers could be anywhere."

"That's true." Professor Powell nodded. "What do you suggest, then?"

"It's simple. We track them and tie them up until we can turn them over to the authorities." He glared at the woods. "These guys aren't ghosts or anything. They're merely other magicals, and I doubt they have as many people as we do. They won't be able to resist us."

"And how are we supposed to track them?" Professor Hudson asked. "There's too much interference for general scrying and tracking spells, and those would require us to at least have some idea where to look."

Raine gasped and snapped her fingers. "You're all making the same mistake Asher and I did when we had our little hide and seek contest."

Everyone turned to look at her, but it was the Wood Elf who asked, "What are you talking about? What mistake?"

She pointed at Cameron's nose, and the boy raised his eyebrows in question.

"Magical interference doesn't mess with the shifter sense of smell," she said. "It'll be easy to distinguish the poachers' scent trails from the mirror cat's. She was killed recently, which means the scent trails will still be strong." She looked at Cameron in query. "Right?"

He nodded. "Unless they went out of their way to hide their scent, that's all true."

Professor Powell gave Raine an approving smile. "That sounds like a good plan. If we rely on Cameron's experience in wolf form, there won't be any confusion like there would be if we depended on olfactory-enhancement spells. This could work."

The shifter nodded. "I'd be happy to help track them."

Asher gave him an appreciative look.

Professor Hudson headed toward the pier. "Regardless of what you all do, I think it's imperative that I contact Fish and Wildlife. I'll go now and try to expedite things, but do whatever you feel is appropriate. You have my support."

Professor Kaylis and Professor Powell both nodded their agreement.

No one spoke for a few moments as she walked toward the pier and a waiting rowboat.

"It's times like this," Professor Kaylis began, "that I can't but help think of Burke. 'The only thing necessary for the triumph of evil is for good men to do nothing.' I don't think any of you want to sit around and do nothing. We all came to this island to survey the major unusual plants and animals here, not to stand by and let them be destroyed. I think we should follow Raine's plan. All of us."

Adrien nodded slowly, an approving look in his eyes.

Professor Powell made deliberate eye contact with each student. "If we go as a group, there will be less risk. None of us professors will tell you that you have to do this or even require you to do it, as there is some danger involved." He looked at Professor Tarelli. "Can you stay here and make sure this site is secure? It might be that they plan to raid the camp to obtain transportation."

The Nyran nodded, a weary look on her face.

"Thank you," he said. "As I was saying, whoever wants to come along with Professor Kaylis and myself is welcome to do so. Those who don't can stay. This isn't technically our responsibility, but Asher is right. If Professor Tarelli is correct and the poachers have the kittens or are about to take them, they might soon leave the island. We have a narrow window to stop them if they haven't already escaped. Anyone who wants to participate, please stand."

Asher was already standing, so Raine was technically the second to find her feet. Cameron stood next, and the other students joined them not long after.

Professor Tarelli cleared her throat. "Perhaps a handful of students could stay in case the poachers do come here."

Silas and Milo walked toward her, determined looks on their faces.

"Excellent," the professor said. She turned to Raine. "Good thinking on the plan, Raine."

The girl blinked, surprised that the Nyran had finally got her name right. "Thank you, Professor."

Professor Powell pointed toward the rowboats. Professor Hudson was already at the pier.

"Let's go find ourselves some poachers," he said.

CHAPTER TWENTY-FOUR

The combined anti-poaching army of the School of Necessary Magic and Orono Academy for Arcane Studies marched through the forest behind Cameron as he sniffed along the trail in wolf form. He had found a strong scent without trouble near the dead mirror cat, but as the group continued through the trees, their eventual destination became increasingly obvious.

"We're almost at the pond," Raine said, her stomach tight. As much as she wanted to catch the poachers, she didn't look forward to a fight with them. She wanted to join the FBI to catch criminals, not engage in magical battles.

Asher scoffed. "They must be using the tunnels Raine saw."

Professor Powell nodded and gestured for Cameron to stop. "It's a possibility, but they might have simply walked past the pond, too. Professor Hudson and I didn't explore the tunnels themselves, only the cave once we verified the existence of the footprints." He exchanged a glance with

Professor Kaylis. "Now that we know where we're going, I'm worried about the island perimeter. We should have thought of that before, especially if the poachers potentially already have what they came for."

The other wizard nodded and scratched his cheek. "I should take a group with me. We can use the boats to make sure they're not already on their way. If anyone spots them, they can release a flare and wait for reinforcements." He pointed to Kelly, Finn, Heidi, Dnai, and Josephine. "I'd like you to come with me. We'll split into three teams. Remember, we're merely looking for them. I don't want anyone to confront them without my help. It's one thing when we're in a group but another when you're students on your own."

The Orono students all nodded, determination on their faces.

Raine wasn't so sure of that. The Orono group might not have fought a chaos witch, but they had experienced their own share of adventures, and Professor Kaylis might have underestimated their ability. Then again, it wasn't like her instructors underestimated the Trouble Squad when they worried about them getting hurt.

She pushed the thoughts away and reminded herself that she wasn't in the FBI yet. That summer, she was still a high schooler, albeit one with a considerable amount of practical experience confronting criminals and dangerous foes.

Professor Kaylis turned to Dnai. "Would you please fly up and keep watch from the air for us, my girl? If you see them, use a flare to let us know where they are. Don't risk yourself by pursuing them too closely."

The girl nodded and started jogging with a casual wave

over her shoulder. "There's a clearing back there where I can get above the canopy."

He nodded to Professor Powell. "We'll leave the rest to you and the remaining students," he said before he turned and walked away. The remaining Orono students, with the exception of Asher, fell in behind him.

Professor Powell gestured ahead. "Okay, everyone else is doing their part to make sure they don't get away, but they might still be ahead of us. Let's move on and see where Cameron's nose takes us."

The wolf released a low growl and lowered his nose to the ground.

***

Cameron shifted into human form at the edge of the water and shook his head. "The trail dead-ends here." He pointed at the muddy terrain. "But the scent was strong right before the water so they probably went in. They might have come out recently, but there's nothing around the edge that would suggest that."

"Then it's definitely the cavern," Raine said. "There's no other alternative."

"You think so, but you can't be sure." Philip stared into the water.

"Why wouldn't they go to the tunnels? Especially if they're worried about someone tracking them.?"

"Because maybe those tunnels don't lead anywhere else. That would explain why we found footprints and scent trails here and why they bothered to cover them up. It's not like they can take kittens through the water."

Asher shrugged. "Why not? If they put them to sleep and used something like an air bubble, it wouldn't be difficult. This might have been deliberate. They might have wanted to make sure their scent couldn't be followed by any mirror cats. If they saw us, they might think it'll be easy to avoid a group of teens and their chaperones."

Sara walked along the edge of the pool and stared at it. "Or they knew we had a shifter with us and were worried about it."

"Should we wait them out?" Evie frowned, obviously uncertain. "Don't they have to come up eventually?"

Adrien kicked the surface in frustration. "Waiting for the enemy means allowing them to set the tempo of battle. I'm sorry, but I don't like the idea."

William looked at Evie with concern.

"They could have set traps or something in there." Evie pointed at the glistening surface of the pond.

"They're here for specific things," the Light Elf said. "This isn't their home."

Raine shook her head. "Adrien's right, and we can't be certain those tunnels don't lead somewhere else anyway. We need to cut their escape routes off." She looked at Professor Powell, unsure that he was still willing to let them help now that they were closer to a confrontation. "The net should slowly tighten around them."

Something approaching a smirk appeared on the wizard's face. She looked away, and a blush suffused her cheeks. Even though their professor and expert in dealing with dark magic was right there, she still reverted to her natural tendency to want to lead her friends against the criminals.

He smiled. "Don't worry, Raine. I agree with you and Adrien. Now that we've committed to this course of action, I believe our only choice is to go into the cavern. Again, anyone who is uncomfortable with the plan is free to stay behind. I would suggest that you return to the boats and take one back to the camp to reinforce Professor Tarelli."

Philip grinned. "Come on, did you really expect the FBI Trouble Squad to want to stay behind?"

"I don't enjoy swimming in strange cloudy ponds, but I'll do it to help catch these guys." William cupped his palm and a small flame appeared.

Professor Powell raised his wand. "I'll do the spell for Cameron. The rest of you, prep shields, air bubbles, and light orbs. We're diving for poachers."

CHAPTER TWENTY-FIVE

The eight students and the professor emerged from the water into the cavern, their clothes soaked. Raine wondered about a tighter-binding spell that would allow them to swim without getting wet at all, but even Professor Powell had used a simple air bubble, which suggested that there weren't simple alternatives.

The drying spell wasn't instant but they didn't have time to worry about discomfort when their quarry might already be halfway to a boat and successful escape.

Evie sighed as she looked around at the luminescent rocks. "It's too bad we don't have time for a tour. This place is pretty. The idea that it's used by poachers makes me sick. This whole island is practically a magical nature preserve, and they come and ruin things."

"That's the thing that lives on a Kraken?" William gestured at one of the floating, buzzing jellyfish.

Philip snickered. "Maybe. She said it lives on large creatures, not necessarily on Kraken."

"We need to stay focused." Raine pointed at the two tunnels.

Professor Powell nodded. "The question is which way do we go?"

Everyone turned to look at Cameron. He shifted and lowered his nose to begin his olfactory search. After a quick growl, he padded forward. The wolf had found the scent again and the poachers wouldn't escape so easily.

Professor Powell, Asher, and Raine walked directly behind him and the other students straggled a few yards back. Everyone's attention was now focused on tracking the criminals and not the glowing rocks on the wall or creatures floating through the air.

Cameron stopped in front of the first tunnel, then walked to the other to sniff for a few seconds. He shook his head and growled again before he returned to the original one and pointed toward it with his muzzle.

"Let's go, then," the professor said. "I doubt Cameron's nose is lying to him. That's our greatest asset for the moment, but only if we take advantage of it right away."

The wolf jogged forward but slowed every few yards to verify the trail. Despite this, they maintained a good pace. The poachers might already be long gone, but at least they were doing their best to catch up.

The tunnel widened after about ten yards. The glowing rocks became more frequent and their light almost rendered the students' orbs unnecessary. Several more jellyfish creatures drifted past and each buzzed at different frequencies. The creatures didn't react at all to the presence of the team.

Their population density increased the farther the

group traveled. The implications of that would have to wait for another day.

Everyone fell silent as they moved deeper, led by the shifter's nose. A few minutes turned into several more, and soon, they had hiked over a mile.

The underground passage split several times into additional forks, but Cameron simply checked the new branches and verified that even if they might hold something interesting—including fourteen-legged crabs scuttling from one—they didn't have a poacher scent. The jellyfish still glided in and out of several of the tunnels, as uninterested in the two-legged visitors as they had been before.

The shaft began to narrow again after several more minutes.

Raine drew slow, deep breaths and wondered if they would stumble upon the poachers or if the criminals had already escaped. She doubted that they were the kind of men who took a slow ferry to the island. All their efforts might be for nothing.

She turned to Professor Powell. "What if—" Her stomach lurched at a now familiar massive pulse of magic. "You have to be kidding me."

The professor pointed his wand up. "Reinforce your shields," he shouted as a massive rumble signaled the start of another earthquake. "Keep moving forward."

Thankfully, she managed to cast her spell only seconds before several rocks detached from the roof and bounced off her shield. A low, rumbling, grinding cacophony echoed through the subterranean passage as the ground shook to jolt the people inside against the walls every few steps. Cameron was the only one who didn't do his best pinball impression. If they hadn't had their shields up, someone would already have broken a bone or worse. Being underground in a confined space during an earthquake might end their quest for the poachers and their lives.

They rushed forward as a group and dodged rocks and occasionally, deflected one with their spells. The dull roar as the earth convulsed grew louder and all-encompassing before a few hearty shakes became slight jostles and finally, a minor tremble.

The quake ended, and everyone sighed with nervous relief as they slowed. Rubble lined much of the tunnel behind them.

"Should we go back?" Philip asked. "In case of another quake?"

"They don't cluster," Raine said. "Or at least they haven't before." She pointed forward. "And we might be closer to an exit now than we were. Turning around will help the poachers and it might not even be the safer plan."

Professor Powell lowered his wand, a determined look on his face. "Raine's right. We've traveled this far already. The best course is to continue. But please, pay attention and refresh your shields as necessary."

Cameron padded ahead of them and sniffed through the debris until he found the trail again. With a hasty nod of his head, he moved forward. The earthquake had startled them, but it hadn't covered the scent. They could still find the poachers—or, if not the poachers themselves, clues that might lead them to the men.

The next few minutes passed in a tense silence in which

everyone seemingly waiting for another magic pulse and an earthquake.

A few happy thoughts filtered into Raine's mind and pushed away some of the dark visions of the possible confrontation ahead. Cameron had told her he was worried because he was a shifter and not someone who could cast spells, but his natural talents were exactly what they needed now. Being able to do more didn't always mean someone was better than those able to do less.

She was proud of him and proud to be his girlfriend.

The sound of running water grew louder as they continued their journey. Raine wasn't sure if that was a good sign or a bad sign. Their tunnel opened into a muddy cavern, its mouth to the outside clearly visible. Stray rays of sunlight filtered through the dense trees beyond the opening. The sound of running water was louder now and echoed off the vast cavern roof.

Several large rocks lay near the tunnel entrance. Most were tall enough to hide the group as long as they crouched.

"I don't know where this is," Professor Powell whispered. "And I'm beginning to wonder if the poachers have been to this island before. They might have raided this place for a while. It's not like it's under constant surveillance. Or they might simply be lucky. Who knows?"

"It doesn't matter," Asher grunted harshly. "All the more reason to capture them, either way. If we don't, they'll wait and come back when they don't think anyone's here."

The group crept forward cautiously. A stream ran past the dense rock formation near the entrance. Several boulders and chunks of rock lay on the ground, victims of the latest earthquake judging by the lack of weathering at several breakpoints.

William's eyes widened, and he pointed into the distance. Three men in dark camouflage outfits with wands in hand ran toward an aluminum skiff. Another was tied to a wooden post only a few yards away.

"We should go now," the Wood Elf hissed. "They're getting away."

Professor Powell shook his head. "No. You're staying."

Raine and Asher both blinked in surprise.

"What?" she said.

He sighed but his expression was firm. "You'll stay here while I pursue them. They don't seem to have the kittens— maybe they never did—but I'll be the one to stop them."

"But we can help," she said and desperation leaked into her voice. "That's why we came."

"It's not that I don't trust your skills and experience, but at the end of the day, you're students. It'd be one thing if we were all on land, but it looks like I'll have to follow them in a boat, and I can't risk you falling overboard. I can't help you against a Kraken and poachers at the same time." The professor darted toward the other boat. "I'll catch them. You stay here and make sure they don't double-back."

He raised his wand as the three figures scrambled into their skiff. The fleeing wizards didn't seem to notice his determined approach. One of the men pointed his wand at the center of the boat and it immediately accelerated away.

Professor Powell lowered his wand and continued to sprint toward the other skiff.

"This is crap," Asher muttered through gritted teeth. "I

can't believe he benched us. We don't have to stand here and take it." He took a step forward.

Raine grabbed his arm and shook her head. "We shouldn't go against what he said. He knows what he's doing, and he'll have a better chance to capture them if he's not distracted and worried about us ending up in the water. I'm not happy about it, but this is about stopping the poachers, not satisfying our egos."

The Wood Elf scoffed. "Whatever." He folded his arms over his chest, his expression belligerent.

The second boat launched rapidly into the stream after the retreating men.

Cameron jogged forward and sniffed the ground. He growled and circled and his nostrils flared as he inhaled deeply. He shook his head a few times.

"What's wrong?" Raine asked.

He shifted into human form and pointed at the rocks and soil below his feet. "The ground's wrong. The scent's wrong, and I'm not sure what it means."

"I don't understand." Raine frowned as she tried to make sense of it.

He pointed toward where the original skiff had been docked. "There's no scent trail leading that way at all. Nothing that smells like the poachers, anyway, to either boat." He pointed in a different direction, which led into the forest. "But there is one leading that way. It's like the poachers went that way and not the way we saw them go."

Sara frowned. "What does that mean? They covered their scent but only part of the time? Maybe we ended up too close behind them so they couldn't pull their normal tricks?"

Raine's eyes widened. "No. It doesn't mean that at all. It's a trick. Don't you see?"

"What kind of trick? Are you saying the scent trail is fake? Something to mislead any mirror cats?"

"No, this trick isn't for cats. It's for us." She raised her wand in front of her face. "My guess is that it was some kind of illusion. Think about it. They tried to hide their scent trails to avoid vengeful cats rather than angry shifters from Charlottesville. An illusion without a scent is something meant to trick people, not cats. They know we're here, and they might even realize how many there are of us. Even the four professors alone is a considerable amount of skilled magic."

"Wait. You're saying Professor Powell's chasing nothing? An illusion?" Asher groaned and slapped a palm to his forehead in frustration.

She lowered her wand and nodded curtly. "Probably. Who knows how long it'll last? It might lead him all the way to the ocean."

The Wood Elf took a few deep breaths and gestured toward the forest where Cameron had pointed before. "If he has a scent trail, we can follow the poachers. If they're trying these illusions, it means we're right on their butts. We need to go now and can't wait around for Powell to figure it out."

"But he told us to stay here," Evie said. "Do you want to go after the poachers without him?"

"The whole point of us being here is to catch them." He jogged toward the forest. "We can send a flare up when we find them. But if we wait here, they'll get away and all of this running around will have accomplished nothing."

"He's right." Raine ran after the elf. Cameron sprinted forward before he shifted into wolf form and bounded ahead.

Adrien chuckled quietly. "It's a good thing Asher and his friends aren't at our school. An expanded FBI Trouble Squad would be a terror to behold." He broke into a jog. "I wonder if it would also mean we'd end up restricted to campus more often."

Sara, Philip, William, and Evie hesitated for a few more seconds before they followed their friends. The FBI Trouble Squad plus one Mainer Monster Hunter were on the case.

CHAPTER TWENTY-SIX

C aution was always useful, but it was most useful ahead of the event. By the time someone stumbled into a situation they hadn't fully prepared for, it was too late. That thought passed through Raine's head as she and her friends stumbled around a tree and into the same three darkly-dressed men they had seen earlier in the cavern. They stood near an identical aluminum skiff already waiting in the stream, and all three had their wands out.

"So it was an illusion," she muttered.

The poachers stood under a huge oak and laughed as if coming back from an entertaining movie or party. There was no zombie moss or glowing mushrooms on the trunk, which appeared to be absolutely normal, to her disappointment. She could have used a little zombie tree help in that moment.

Several caged mirror cats meowed plaintively. Another cage contained a stump covered in the zombie moss. A variety of birds—some colorful and others quite mundane —were caged as well.

Raine drew a deep breath. The men couldn't escape, no matter what. Even with Dnai and the other students patrolling the perimeter, the culprits might slip through with the help of a spell.

"Stop right there," she shouted because she really had no idea what else to do. She pointed her wand at the men. "Drop your wands and put your hands on your head."

Still in wolf form, Cameron moved in front of her and growled. Sara's hand lowered to her pouch, and Evie drew a red-colored potion in a rectangular vial from her pocket. Flames appeared in William's hand. Philip glared at the men, while Asher raised his hands. A satisfied smile spread over Adrien's face as a sword winked into existence.

One of the poachers smirked at Raine. "Who the hell are you supposed to be? The Magical Scouts of America? You kids should be careful playing with those kinds of toys if you don't want to end up hurt."

"We're the people who will stop you," she responded sharply. "Surrender, and you won't be hurt. We'll restrain you and wait for the proper authorities to drag you off to jail so you can reflect on your crimes. Your little illusion trick was cute, but we saw right through it."

The criminal's face twitched. "Did you now?" He scoffed and glared at his companions. "I told you we shouldn't have done it."

"Now, about that surrender…" She shook her wand in her best attempt at menace.

He laughed and gestured toward her with his wand. "Get a hold of Sergeant Girl Scout here. Listen, girly, you and your little friends and your pet wolf there had better back off if you don't want to get hurt. We don't feel generous given that we spent a lot of time planning a pick-up only to find you and your parents sniffing around. You ruined what should have been a milk-run. That causes me a lot of stress, and when I am stressed out, somebody has to pay for it."

Cameron's lip curled around his long, low growl.

The poacher responded with a smirk.

Asher snorted. "They aren't our parents. Those are our professors. We're from the Orono Academy for Arcane Studies and the School of Necessary Magic, two of the best magic schools in this country. We represent the Magical Multitudes Project, and we're here to protect the animals."

"Have you ever killed anyone, elf boy? Huh?" Their adversary gave him a toothy grin. "I have, and I think the black-market value of those mirror cats alone is worth a few lives."

The Wood Elf shook his head. "You don't scare me."

"Then you're as stupid as you are young."

Adrien stared coldly at the men. "Don't be so certain about the battle experience of your enemies based on our age. You have no idea about the kind of foes we've faced in the past."

Raine wrinkled her nose in disgust. "You're a sociopath. Surrender already. I really don't want to have to hurt you, but we won't allow you to escape."

"This ain't school, kids. This is the real world." He glared menacingly. "And in the real world, it's all about taking what you want when you want. So, this is your last chance. I ain't never killed a kid before, but there's nothing to say I can't start today."

Asher laughed, which drew confused looks from both the other students and the criminals.

"What's so funny, elf boy?" the man demanded. "I don't think you realize the trouble you're in."

"No, you moron. You don't realize the trouble you're in." Asher nodded at Raine. "She's not only a witch in magic school. She's training to be the first FBI witch. The guy with the fire hands will also join the FBI." He gestured to Adrien. "He's training to be a Guardian, and I'm partial to becoming a game warden now after seeing all this." He inclined his head toward Philip. "That guy is obsessed with public service, and you're ruining his summer." With a last flick of his arm, he pointed at Evie. "And she's already a better potions witch than half the country, even though she's only a teen. You picked the wrong group to try to poach out from under. So, give up right now."

Their opponent narrowed his eyes. His gaze shifted from one student to the other as he licked his lips and new tension lined his features. "FBI trainees? Guardians? Are you kidding me?" He uttered a string of profanities so complicated, it could have been an incantation. "Just our luck. But that don't change anything."

Raine squared her shoulders. "Yes, it does. It's like my friend said. We've taken on many more impressive people than you. We fought the Witch Queen of Chaos."

"I've had enough of this garbage. Don't cry to me when you get hurt." The poacher snapped his wand up and shouted an incantation. A fireball blasted from it toward her.

She dropped instantly, not sure how much her shield

would protect her, and muttered a restraining spell as she landed. A rope appeared and spun toward the poacher.

He whipped his wand in a circle, a sneer on his face. The rope sliced in half and fell harmlessly.

The truth was that the team were at a disadvantage in that killing their opponents was less of an option, but even though her heart pounded, her stomach didn't tighten with fear. They had the training, experience, and will to win, exactly like they had so many times before.

Adrien circled to the side of the criminals. He jogged casually as if they were merely out doing team conditioning, a tight smile on his face.

The other two men spaced themselves on either side of their leader and launched fireball attacks of their own. William thrust in front of Evie and hissed when his defenses absorbed one of the strikes.

Philip pointed his wand at the feet of one of the men. His digging spell shunted dirt and twigs into a cloud in front of the wizard and blinded him for a moment. The poacher ceased his attack.

Sara hurled one of her few acorns toward the boat and Evie lobbed a potion a moment later. The seeds found their target and erupted into a shower of wooden spikes to pierce the craft. A few seconds later, Evie's potion struck the side and detonated, ripping a hole in the side.

"Woah." Evie blinked. "I guess I used too much after all."

"No!" screamed the first poacher. "I will *kill* you for that."

Asher raised his arms toward an oak tree and whispered a spell. A branch dropped and smacked the wand out of one of the poacher's hands before it wound around him.

He shouted and struggled but was soon snuggly secured by the non-zombie tree.

Cameron rocketed forward with loud growls and snarls.

Raine rolled onto her knees and conjured an ice wall to absorb the constant fireball barrages.

William thrust his palm out and launched a white-hot flame bolt at the arm of the other active poacher. The man grunted and stumbled back. A faint shimmer indicated a shield, but his wince proved that it hadn't saved him entirely.

Sara threw a seed and an acorn toward the enemy. Both men obliterated the incoming kitsune missiles with cones of flame.

"That's not fair!" she shouted.

Philip raised a slab of dirt in time to protect her from twin fireballs.

She smiled at him. "Good timing."

"I have my moments." He winked.

Another branch lowered from the tree, but this time, the criminals were ready for it and sliced it away with a quick spell. The second man began quick-firing small fire-balls toward the students like a machine gun, while his leader used a few seconds to chant a spell.

Raine couldn't make it out from where she stood, but she didn't have to wait long. A large translucent blade extended from his wand. With a yell, he spun and sliced through the trunk of the tree.

"Are you nuts?" Asher demanded.

The wizard grinned as the mighty oak toppled. It crashed over the stream with a thunderous rumble and the bulk of it splashed into the water with a violent eruption of water. The man rushed toward it and hopped on the end.

His partner, who had laid down cover fire, glanced at him with a frown. Cameron barreled into the distracted man and knocked him off his feet. His wand spun away from him.

Adrien closed on the disabled and trapped poachers, a faint look of disappointment now on his face. He shrugged and used a quick burst to hurtle toward their fleeing leader, his sword raised high.

"You will not escape," the Light Elf shouted.

The poacher threw his arm up and launched a fireball at him.

The elf grunted in pain as he tumbled past the man and landed hard. His shield protected him from the worst of the attack, although his slightly charred shirt would serve as a reminder. He pushed to his feet, his sword still in hand, to face his adversary.

The poacher hesitated and looked around, uncertainty on his face. "This is ridiculous. You're only a group of kids."

Raine and Philip advanced toward him, their wands pointed and ready. Sara clutched another couple of seeds and narrowed her eyes. Evie rubbed a golden potion in a glass vial between her fingers, anger on her face. William held fire in both hands as he advanced, his face a grim mask. Asher had positioned himself on their far flank. He held his hand out, a slight smirk on his face.

Cameron remained on top of the fallen poacher and continued to growl menacingly into his face.

"You've lost," Raine said, her wand still pointed at their quarry. "And you've lost badly, despite the fact that we didn't want to seriously hurt you. You tried to kill us and you failed, and you'll answer for your crimes."

Asher slammed his fist into palm. "To be honest, I do want to seriously hurt you, but I'd rather see you rot in jail."

Adrien pointed his sword at the poacher. "You can continue to fight, of course. But now, you're badly outnumbered whereas before, you were merely outnumbered. Do you really think you can win against eight highly trained students with battle experience?"

The poacher jerked his head as if in search of an escape and sweat dotted his brow. Finally, he dropped his wand, fell to his knees, and stuck his hands behind his head. "This is insane. I can't believe we were beat by a bunch of kids."

Raine shook her head and smiled. "It's like my friend said. We're not simply anyone, we're students of two great magical schools, and we've had considerable practical field experience if you want to call it that." She pointed her wand to the sky and with a quick incantation, launched a flare. "And if you think we're scary, wait until you meet our professors."

CHAPTER TWENTY-SEVEN

The small boat that carried the arrested poachers sailed away from the pier and Raine smiled with real satisfaction. Professor Hudson had actually managed to get the authorities there in hours. Apparently, they took poaching on a protected magical island much more seriously than anyone—even the four professors—anticipated. Technically, New Firefly Island was a restricted zone, so that might have fueled their resolve.

The exact reasons didn't matter. The important thing was that the men would pay for their crimes. Before, they only had to worry about poaching and trespassing charges, but now, they also faced a variety of other charges, not the least of which was attempted murder.

She sighed quietly. Sometimes, she wondered if it was a bad thing to be so inured to the danger she and her friends had experienced, but she chose to view it as something that would be helpful in her FBI service. She had already seen darkness, chaos, and violence, and she understood how law enforcement could protect people who couldn't otherwise protect themselves.

Professor Kaylis cleared his throat behind her.

Raine turned with a smile. Most of the students had gathered around the firepit. The setting sun left the sky a beautiful orange-red, but something about her FBI instincts had made her want to see the criminals off. It filled her with satisfaction, and she couldn't wait to talk to Agent Connor about everything that had happened.

Professor Powell stepped onto the path leading from the camp to the pier, but he was still dozens of yards away.

"An excellent job, Raine," Professor Kaylis said with a smile. "I've told the others, but I wanted to let you know they'll do a better job of monitoring the island going forward. That much was made clear. They might not be able to use drones here, but they can use them around it. I think also...but perhaps I'm reading too much into it."

"Reading too much into what?" she asked.

"I think the paradigm has shifted concerning New Firefly Island with the loss of the mirror cat mother."

She frowned in confusion. "Paradigm? What do you mean?"

"You have to understand, Raine. Before, I'm fairly certain that the government was far more concerned about people getting hurt by the animals living on this island rather than the opposite. Indeed, one of the goals of the Magical Multitudes Project is to evaluate the potential impact of magical creatures on the environment and people around them, but it was all theoretical. This place... the biodiversity..." He smiled gently, a satisfied expression on his face. "Now that we've so clearly established that there are many rare species here, it'll change many things. Even the magic complicates the situation. However, there are still several relevant laws protecting rare and endangered species, so I doubt they'll have a problem with poachers again."

She returned her gaze to the ocean and the receding boat. "That's good to hear. I would hate to think students on a geology trip next year would have to face a group of poachers."

Professor Kaylis chuckled. "Indeed. I can see how that would be a problem." He waved a hand in an expansive gesture. "Anyway, I have personally thanked each student who was involved in stopping those men. I'm proud to have worked with you this summer, and I look forward to hearing more about your accomplishments in the future." He offered her a final nod before he turned to leave.

Professor Powell passed the other man and stopped in front of her. "How do you feel? I could tell you were a little obsessed with stopping those men."

"I feel much better and definitely satisfied. Very satisfied." Raine shrugged and looked down. "Are you angry that we didn't stay where you told us to? It's mostly my fault that we left."

"Funny. Asher claimed it was mostly his fault, and everyone else made it clear that it was their decision." He chuckled. "As your instructor, I should say yes, of course I'm angry you disobeyed my order, but let's be honest. The point of going to the School of Necessary Magic isn't to learn to follow orders. It's to bring out the best of your magical ability." He placed a hand over his heart. "I let myself be fooled, and you all saw through that and stopped those men. The situation I thought was in play actually wasn't. It would have been foolish to blindly follow my order after that. This incident merely reinforces our belief in you."

"Your belief?"

"Yes. You only have a year left in our school, and I'm honestly not sure how much more we have to teach someone like you. While we can teach you new spells, new techniques, and new history, you already have the key part of what it means to be a good witch and you prove that constantly semester after semester." He offered her a wry smile. "Now, you've even proved it in the summer."

Raine shook her head. "I want to be clear that it wasn't only me. It was all my friends, including Asher. I wouldn't have been able to stop those men on my own. Everything I've accomplished here has only been because other people have helped me."

"You say that like it's a bad thing."

"I only want to make sure everyone gets the credit they deserve."

Professor Powell nodded. He glanced up as a pair of seagulls glided above them. "And I'm glad you're doing that and appreciate how important your friends are, but you need to realize how special you are, even without friends."

"I'm a normal witch. I'm not powerful or even the best at technique."

"Power is one thing, but it's only one aspect—and so is magic, for that matter. Leadership's important, Raine. Very important, especially in a world as complicated as ours that will take the next few centuries to resolve all its issues." He pointed at her. "Understanding how to rally a team is an important skill, one that can't always be taught, even to smart people. Let's be realistic. As an example, Evie is a naturally gifted potions witch, but do you see her as a leader?" He raised an eyebrow. "Be honest."

She averted her gaze. "She doesn't need to be a leader."

"I'm not saying she does, and I'm not trying to insult her either. The world needs potions witches, just as it needs leaders. The truth I want you to see is that you're a natural-born leader, Raine, with a fine moral sense that has been cultivated by your parents and your guardians." Professor Powell gazed at the horizon, a pained look in his eyes. "The darkness is always there, waiting, so it's especially important that we have people on the side of light—people like you, Raine. The magical community couldn't ask for a better first representative in the FBI. I'm proud to have done my small part in your magical education."

Raine looked down as her face heated. She took a few deep breaths before responding. "T-Thank you, Professor Powell, but the only reason we've been able to do most of the things we've done is because of all the quality education we've received. The things you've taught us in your class alone have saved our lives. Professor Hudson's classes have helped me understand my place in the world along with a lot of other magicals, which has helped me to not always make ignorant mistakes like I would have before coming to the School of Necessary Magic."

His gloom vanished with a grin. He turned to look at the lightly churning ocean. "I'm glad to hear that, even if I do pride myself on providing a rather pragmatic and directly applicable magical education. I would hate to think I've taught nothing but useless spells." He nodded toward the camp. "You should get back if only so Cameron will relax. I think he's half-convinced you'll swim to the mainland to look for more crimes to solve."

"No, I think that scratched my itch for the summer." She released a contented sigh. "Will we be able to stay on the island? We're still supposed to have several weeks, and now that the poachers have been caught, we can explore that cavern. I'm not only obsessed with crime, you know. I want to learn."

"That's always a good thing, and one of the reasons Leo likes you so much." The professor's grin faded slowly. "But, well, I'll be honest. We're unsure whether we'll be able to complete our stay here."

"Why?" Raine shook her head. "We removed the main threat."

"We removed a threat, yes, but not all threats." He pointed to the mazeball court in the distance. "We might have to leave for the same reason that we don't want you to play on that—those earthquakes. Once we learned there might be poachers here, it occurred to us that they might somehow be responsible, especially because of the magical pulses, but it's very clear now that they weren't. Something else is going on with this island, and if we can't understand it, we might have to leave until somebody identifies the issue and stabilizes it. Right now, the tremors can be dealt with through the use of quick magic, but if they worsen even slightly, it could end up as a serious situation and with someone hurt."

She sighed and her shoulders slumped. "So are we leaving or not?"

Professor Powell shook his head. "Not yet. Not unless

things get worse, but I did want you to understand that the situation could change in an instant."

"We should definitely explore the cavern and tunnels while we still have a chance then." She flung a hand in the vague direction of the pond. "There have to be cool things in there. Maybe we can find the Kraken—if there is one."

He nodded toward the campsite. "Not everyone will want to go in a cavern. I'm not sure it's safe." He laughed. "And although I doubt there's a Kraken around here that has somehow escaped the Navy's attention, you should avoid it if you do find one."

Raine grinned. "Fair enough. As for people not wanting to go, we might be missing out on rare species, and if we don't have the poachers to worry about, we can break into smaller teams again, right?"

"I suppose you are not only a leader, but you're also stubborn. That can be a disadvantage at times but being able to stick to what you want often leads to you achieving it. I'll talk to the other professors. I'm sure we can work something out. How does that sound?"

She smiled. "Thank you. That's all I ask."

"You're welcome, Raine." Professor Powell turned and started down the pier. "And keep up the good work."

CHAPTER TWENTY-EIGHT

Raine tilted her head as she crept down the narrow rocky path with Cameron at her side. The pale glow from several of the rocks almost made her light orb unnecessary. The tunnel system didn't look any different than it had previously. She thought it might somehow be more inviting now that the poachers were gone, but the same sense of heavy mystery clung to it.

At least now that they knew about the entrance on the other side, it made the process of entry far less troublesome and easier on the shifter too. The idea of layering spells and swimming with such a short, ticking time limit seemed more bizarre than it had before now that she had time to actually think about it.

Much of what had happened during the last few weeks seemed strange in hindsight. She had been caught up in the relaxed atmosphere of the summer research trip and somehow, that almost made poachers and mysterious earthquakes not seem like a big deal at the time, even though she'd had to fight for her life against men prepared to murder her and her friends.

"I can't believe Professor Powell actually let us go by ourselves," she said. "I wish Philip, Sara, and Evie could come, but I understand that Evie really wanted to help with the botanical survey of those flowers that Dnai spotted when she was looking for the poachers." She smiled. "It's funny how good things can come out of bad things."

He grunted acknowledgment. "The initial surveys and maps aren't that great. I don't expect millimeter accuracy or anything, but I would have thought they would have put a little more effort into it."

"They didn't really need to. After all, many people like us are coming to help with the island."

Cameron snickered. "By the way, I think the reason Professor Powell let us go by ourselves is that this is his way to reward you by giving you quality time with your boyfriend." He tapped his forehead. "He knows how you think. You want to keep busy, but you don't want to neglect your friends or me, so he set it up."

"Did he say that?" Her expression was more than a little dubious.

"No, but that's the feeling I had. Why? Is it a problem?"

Raine rolled her eyes. "Of course it's not a problem. I simply wasn't sure with all the earthquake talk."

"Yeah, that's the other thing. I think that's the other reason he wanted it to be me and you."

"How do you mean?

"When you do your Raine of Arc speeches and convince everyone to do something dangerous, I'm the one who will most likely still concentrate on making sure you're not hurt. All the professors understand that. He does too." He shrugged. "I think he's that way with the headmistress. They have a similar relationship vibe."

She laughed. "You think you understand their relationship vibe?"

"Sure." The shifter grinned. "Call it animal instinct. That's why I think I get along so well with Professor Powell lately. Our girlfriends are both stubborn, talented women who spend too much time concerned about everyone but themselves."

"There are worse things than being compared to Headmistress Berens." She slowed as they closed on a twisting pathway that provided a choice between two different directions. "And, by the way, Raine of Arc?" She rolled her eyes. "I don't talk people into dangerous stuff. I'm only dedicated to helping people out. If everyone wants to come along and help me, I won't turn them down. There's nothing wrong with helping people."

"I know. I know." Cameron put both hands in front of his chest. "And you'd be a crappy FBI agent if you didn't care about helping people. I'm just saying. Hey, you know what it's like?"

"What?"

"It's like when you fly. It doesn't matter where you're going or whether it's subsonic or supersonic. They all give you that same safety speech—the part where they say you should put your oxygen mask on first before helping anybody else?"

Raine sighed. "It's not the same thing."

"It totally is." He mimed putting on a mask. "Which is

why I need to be around to make sure you have the stupid mask on, and that's why we're here now in the dark tunnels looking for...something." He ran his hands along the moist rock of the wall. "I have to say, though, all we've found so far is jellyfish and more glowing rock. There might not be anything else down here to find. You have to at least consider that possibility."

She grinned at him. "Oh, what? You're saying you don't want to spend hours wandering underground caverns in dim lighting with your girlfriend? I would have thought most boys would think that was a great time."

"Being together with your girlfriend, yes. Wandering caves and tunnels, no," Cameron scoffed. "It's not like we're making out, and I wouldn't want to do that in this slime and jellyfish factory anyway. This place doesn't exactly scream romantic mood."

"I'm not here for romance." She laughed. "There's something here. Something else we can find. We're supposed to survey this island for rare creatures and plants. It doesn't hurt to examine the inside in addition to the surface."

The shifter frowned. "How can you be sure there's something to find? The poachers didn't mention anything about it, and they obviously used these tunnels more than a little."

"The poachers didn't care." Raine tapped her wand against the wall. "The cavern and tunnel system were merely ways for them to get from point A to point B. They were looking for easy money, not the answers to hidden questions. Do you really think that guy and his cronies are the kind of people who feel wonder and awe at unexplained mysteries?"

"No." He stopped and frowned. "Wait."

Raine halted immediately. "What is it? Do you hear something?"

He shook his head. "No, but now that you mention it—and I'd forgotten about it—the other day when we followed the scent trails, there was one path that smelled weird. I can't say I've ever smelled anything like it. In fact, it was so strange, I can't even put the smell into words."

She put her hands on her hips and fixed him with a stern look. "And you're only telling me this now? That screams 'I'm a mystery, solve me!' Are you trying to mess with me?"

"I didn't care at the time. All I cared about was tracking the poachers. Anything that wasn't related to them might as well have been a million years in the future. There are many scents around this island and I needed to focus." He shrugged. "And then we had the fight and the agents came, and the professors had their questions after that. It was one thing after another. It wasn't like I tried to keep it from you."

"Well, the important thing is that you've told me now." She pointed her wand back the way they had come and the soft light of her orb gave her face a vaguely sinister cast. "Do you at least remember where you smelled that weird scent? It might be nothing, or it could be the hidden artifact that changes everything we know about Oriceran."

"I doubt that it's anything like that, but I do remember the general area where I smelled it." He cracked his knuckles. "This should be easy. I'll lead you there, shift, and we can follow the scent until I find the secret KFC recipe or whatever is down there."

She gave him a calm nod but her heart raced a little. There had to be something important. It was time once again for the evidence to lead the case.

———

Cameron padded quietly in wolf form with Raine behind him. They'd followed the unusual scent trail for twenty minutes and had taken so many turns and twists, there was no way she would ever be able to navigate back to the original tunnel without his help.

Aside from their breathing and the drip of water, only oppressive silence filled the tunnels.

She sighed.

He looked at her over his shoulder, his head cocked, and whined inquisitively.

"It's annoying that you can't talk." She shrugged. "I don't want to only hear my own voice."

His rumbling half-growl doubled as wolf laughter.

"I know that you're leading us there using your wolf senses, but our time together is so precious that I feel like I'm wasting it by not being able to talk to you." She shrugged.

The shifter's ears lowered, and he whined quietly.

"I know, I know. I'm not being reasonable. Do you think we're close at least?"

He nodded.

"Oh, that's not so bad then." Raine managed a smile. "Maybe it's something really exotic, like the tomb of the most ancient gnome."

Cameron looked behind at her, his stare a little disconcerting.

"I'm not saying that's a thing. But maybe something like that. We'll see soon enough."

A few more minutes of travel passed, which included two more turns, before they approached a vast, pulsating chamber. The closer they moved, the heavier the weight of massive amounts of magic that hung over her. Her theory about a powerful artifact might not have been as crazy as she'd thought.

The wolf shifted into human form and stepped in front of her before they entered the cavern.

Her breath caught as they stepped inside. Outside, the heavy levels of magic were plainly obvious, but inside, the intense magical pressure that flowed over her was unlike she'd ever felt. While she understood her experiences were limited compared to someone like Librarian Decker, she'd at least been in a couple of kemanas and unusual magic situations, and this didn't feel at all comparable. Like her boyfriend, she had no true point of reference for what she sensed.

The walls, ceiling, and much of the floor of the dome-shaped area were encrusted with small, irregular nodules of iridescent rock. A slow, pulsing cerulean glow from the nodules provided illumination, but there didn't seem to be anything that remotely resembled an artifact.

Raine licked her lips and rubbed her shoulder. "I know you can't feel it, but the magic in here is crazily high. It's like being shoved directly into the charged quartz of a kemana or gobbling aventurine. No—injecting it directly into your veins. I feel like I could do major magic right now. With this kind of power, I could have probably flung those three poachers to Antarctica with one spell."

Cameron frowned as he turned slowly. He gestured to the walls and the ceiling. "I'll tell you what I think. This isn't a natural formation. The shape's too regular, even if these weird glowing rocks seem to be vaguely random. It's like someone formed this room with a particular purpose." He shrugged. "Or it grew that way. I don't know. But it doesn't look like something you'd get from rocks simply shifting or falling or even eroding. You'd know better than I would."

"What are you saying? That it's a secret kemana or something hidden on this island?" Raine leaned forward to peer more closely at one of the nodules. "This doesn't look like quartz or a quartz-related mineral, but I'm not a hundred percent sure what you can charge and what you can't, so maybe it is some kind of magical battery." She tapped her bottom lip, her mind racing. "If there is a secret kemana here, that might explain the earthquakes. Maybe there's an artifact or something that goes off because of the magic from this place. We only have to find it."

"That could be it." He shrugged. "Like I said, you would know better than I would. No one seems to think the earthquakes are natural, so that's as good an explanation as any. But if it is an artifact, just because it's powered by this room doesn't mean we'll be able to find it."

"Maybe." She frowned as she peered hopefully at their surroundings. "Do you know what I don't see? Something I'd expect if this is kind sort of kemana."

"Hap and some Willen in red coats?"

She chuckled. "No. There's nothing marked anywhere.

No glyphs, no messages, and no sign that this is anything other than a weird room. I can feel the power, but that's it. The kemanas were mostly built before the gates closed the last time. People understood that they would be around for thousands of years. If this is supposed to be something like that, why would it be here on some random island in Maine with no indication of what its purpose is?"

"You got me." Cameron reached toward one of the nodules. "I wonder what this feels like." He ran his thumb over a few. "It's surprisingly smooth."

Raine collapsed to her knees as magic blasted through her. Her stomach lurched, and she vomited. The room pulsed brighter and the light turned blinding in intensity. The shifter grunted as he slid an arm around her to take her weight and prevent her from falling.

Her eyes rolled toward the back of her head. "It's coming. An earthquake's coming."

The room shook violently. The last thing she saw before she passed out was Cameron lifting her into his arms.

"You'll be all right, Raine. I'll get us out of here. You can trust me."

CHAPTER TWENTY-NINE

She groaned as her eyes flickered open in her bed in her cabin. Professors Hudson and Powell stood over her, concerned looks on their faces. Cameron stood in the corner, his arms folded and a scowl on his face.

"What happened?" she mumbled.

"You passed out," the shifter said. "I touched one of those weird rocks in that chamber, and it caused an earthquake somehow. It was too close. Luckily, I remembered the way out. I don't have magic and I couldn't have dug us out of there."

"But why did I pass out?"

Professor Hudson patted her hand. "Because you were too close to a major concentration of leaking magic. Don't worry. It won't result in any lasting harm, even if the earthquake it caused was nasty."

Professor Powell wore a grim look. "It was one of the strongest yet and several of the cabins were damaged. We repaired them, but that means this island could have earthquakes strong enough to collapse the structures, which in turn means it's not safe here anymore."

Raine sat up. Her stomach still felt like someone had used it for origami practice. "But now we know the cause. Someone can go there and determine how to stop the earthquakes, right?"

"Maybe." He shrugged. "Sometimes, knowing the cause and being able to stop it are two completely different things, especially when it comes to magic. I'm sorry, Raine. That's often the way things are."

The cabin door flung open, and Professor Tarelli charged through the opening, wild-eyed. "I want to use an opposite-eye potion on Raine. Right now."

Cameron stepped in front of her, his eyes flashing yellow.

Raine blinked. "Opposite eye? Isn't that like a memory extraction potion?"

The Nyran shook her head. "No, no, Jessie, it's not like that at all. Mostly."

She sighed. So much for the professor knowing her name. "Can you clarify exactly what it does, then?"

Professor Hudson stepped forward and cleared her throat quietly. "Its effects are limited. You can see people's memories, but that's it. You literally see what they saw, and they retain the memory. You don't hear what they heard or know what they thought." She turned toward the wide-eyed Professor Tarelli. "That magic can be rather exhausting, and she just went through a rather unpleasant experience. Why do you need to use it?"

The other woman threw her hand up. "This is important. Very important. Extremely important." She pointed at

Cameron without looking at him. "Especially since I think I know what he described—or, at least, what the others told me he described." She rubbed the back of her neck as if to release the tension that defined her. "Opposite-eye will let me confirm it."

"And what is that?" Professor Hudson asked.

"No, no, no. I'm not saying anything. You might mock me if I say it. Let me do the spell. That way I don't *think*, I *know*, and then we can all share in the joy of such wonderful discovery."

The shifter frowned. "If you need to see what someone there saw, do the spell on me. I didn't pass out."

"I can't. I wish I could, but it doesn't work on shifters." The professor shrugged. "Call it a quirk of anatomy, genetics, or merely some aspect of your anti-magic nature. I don't know. I really don't care, to be honest. Right now, I'm only interested in seeing what Raine saw. Either you take me to that cavern so I can see for myself, or I use the potion."

"Just do it," Raine said. "If it's that important, I don't mind being uncomfortable. I'm sure Professor Tarelli wouldn't ask if it wasn't for a good reason."

The look on the other two professor's faces suggested that they didn't agree with that assessment.

The Nyran woman clapped her hands together. "Good girl. I knew you would side with championing knowledge." She yanked a potion out of a pocket of her khaki shorts, twisted the cap off, and swallowed half the contents before she handed it to the girl. "Focus on the cavern you passed out in. I don't care about anything else. Only that cave."

Raine brought the potion to her lips and closed her

eyes. She imagined the strange pulsating cavern in her mind's eye as she downed the potion. The thick liquid slid down her throat and she gagged and almost threw up again at its awful smell—like a mixture of old socks and a garbage dump.

Pain spiked through her head, and she understood why people didn't like it. She gritted her teeth and struggled to focus on the chamber.

"I have it." Professor Tarelli slapped something cool and smooth in Raine's hand.

She opened her eyes. It was another potion in a small glass vial.

"Take that," the professor said. "It'll end the spell and the unpleasant side-effects."

She opened the potion and swallowed the contents eagerly. It didn't taste any better going down, but her headache stopped instantly. She would take the small victories.

Professor Tarelli took several steps back until she encountered the wall, her eyes wide. She stared at Raine and her mouth hung open. "Everything makes sense now. Everything makes perfect sense. I even suspected it, but I thought, no, it couldn't be that, because it's ridiculous even by the standards of this strange island. But I saw it because you saw it, and now, the truth is there and I can't deny it, no matter how much it hurts my brain to admit it."

Professor Powell frowned. "Can you be a little clearer on what you're talking about? Raine is suffering because of whatever happened down there, and we still have to address the problem of the earthquakes before this island destroys itself or we evacuate."

"No, no." She shook a finger that trembled with suppressed excitement. "Not earthquakes."

He scoffed. "Yes, those were definitely earthquakes."

"No, that wasn't plates shifting and ground moving. Sure, that happens, but it's better to think of it as a frown or a disapproving growl." The woman growled as if to clarify the point.

Cameron strode forward and glared at her. "Will you explain what the heck is going on? What did you see? Explain it!"

She laughed quietly. "The truth, Kyle. Oh—wait, is it Christopher?" She waved a hand vaguely. "No matter. It's not important right now." She rounded on the glaring Professor Powell. "It's a mallaoch. It was an internal inclusion from a mallaoch."

The man stumbled back as if punched. Professor Hudson paled.

"That's impossible," Professor Powell said, his face a mask of pure confusion and denial. "That's completely impossible."

The shifter snarled with rising impatience. "What's a mallaoch?"

Raine nodded quickly. Everyone seemed keyed into the truth except her and her boyfriend, and they were the ones who had seen the stupid cavern.

Professor Powell cut through the air with his hand. "You can't know it's a mallaoch. There's no way one could be on Earth." His tone suggested a combination of confusion and outrage.

Professor Tarelli giggled. "Except what Raine saw matches an internal node exactly. Trust me. I've memorized what they look like from the records in the Great Library." She rounded on Raine. "No one alive has ever seen one, and that includes the gnomes of the Great Library. Still, there are books that relate information about these creatures that are so rare and wonderous, even many Oricerans believe they are mere legend." She threw a hand up to cut Cameron off as he opened his mouth. "New Firefly Island isn't merely a boring island. It's a mallaoch. They are massive creatures native to Oriceran oceans. Tens of thousands of years ago, they were more common, but they were rare even then. Most died even before the Great War, and that little event certainly didn't help the few remaining. You have to understand. They aren't simply rare. They're rare, rare, rare. Super-rare. All but extinct."

Raine blinked several times. "I don't understand. You're saying the island is alive?"

"No. Not at all. That would be silly. Well, depending on the circumstances. In some cases, it might not be silly, but in this case, it is. The island itself isn't a living animal." Professor Tarelli shifted from one leg to the other like an excited child about to open a present. "I can't even begin to imagine how one might have ended up outside Maine. The only possibility is that it came over when the gates were last fully open, and maybe in the cycle before that. But how and why?"

"The cycle before that?" Cameron shook his head, disbelief now mingled with his anger. "How long do these things live?"

"Their lifespan is so vast, even gnomes are like mayflies to them." Professor Tarelli's breath caught, and she pointed at Raine. "It also explains why there is this strange combination of so many rare species that aren't always together. It must have been the previous cycle, not the one before. They creatures accompanied the mallaoch when it came to Earth from Oriceran. Wait. No. That still doesn't quite answer why they are here. The combination of species is still unusual, and it would have been even then. Huh. I still have to think about this."

Raine rubbed her temples. "Can we get back to what this thing is? Is it some kind of giant creature that effectively lives forever?"

"Oh, the simplest way to think of it is that's a massive creature made mostly of...well, I suppose you would say stone and minerals. They tend to generate islands around themselves with magic. It's rather like a shell. In ancient times on Oriceran, some people even worshipped them and sought to purposefully live on one."

The shifter dropped onto the edge of a bed. "So this island is the shell of this super-creature, and it's what? Angry that we're here? That's why we have the earthquakes?"

The professor shook her head. "They aren't intelligent as we would usually define it, but they are highly empathic and they have a natural ability with powerful magic, as you've encountered. I suspect the increased earthquakes before were in reaction to the actions of the poachers. It's inevitable that there will be some minor quakes on a mallaoch island simply because of certain basic processes of life. That said, you have to understand that the creature itself doesn't really perceive individual organisms like you and I as actual entities, but with enough pain and suffering, something becomes an irritant, and it can react to that.

That's why the quakes grew stronger. Increased and prolonged suffering triggered it, not the quick death of predator and prey or the natural cycle of life."

Raine took several deep breaths. "A living island."

"Of sorts. That's accurate enough for now. Maybe."

She stared at the professor. "And, what? Cameron basically tickled its throat earlier?"

Professor Tarelli laughed. "A somewhat accurate metaphor. Yes, that chamber is the equivalent of one of its internal organs. He tickled from the inside, and it wanted to throw up, I suppose you could say." Her smile disappeared. "The only thing I still don't understand is how it actually got to Earth. People are right to be skeptical in that regard. For all their powerful magic, they have no ability with portal magic. It wouldn't even occur to such a creature to create something like a portal to Earth. I wonder if this has something to do with the random species distribution. There has to be a connection." She paced in the small cabin and almost bumped into Cameron and the other two professors, although she showed no sign that she was even aware of it.

Professor Hudson smiled gently. "I have a theory that might explain that."

The Nyran woman stopped and pointed at the witch. "Your theory, please. I welcome it."

"Do you know the history of our school?"

She shook her head. "Not particularly. I know it was established after the gates started opening. What about it?"

"Tucker Underwood, the previous Fixer, donated the land we use."

"That's very nice of him." She nodded quickly. "Very

nice. I've never met a fixer, former or current, but I'd like one if they gave me land."

"That's less important than the fact that he has spent considerable time preserving magical species." Professor Hudson smiled at Raine. "And he's not the only Oriceran to ever have that idea. What if thousands of years ago, there was someone who had the same idea? Someone who wanted to preserve rare species and decided they would save one of the rarest of all by sending it to another world where it could act as a living nature preserve? They might have even done it because of the Great War."

Professor Tarelli tapped the side of her head. "Hmm. That might work. Obviously, the mallaoch has enough natural magic or absorbed enough that it's—" She gasped. "It was probably hibernating before the gates opened. Enough to keep itself alive, and all the while, the animals and plants on it continued to live as usual, self-sustaining over the eons."

Raine shook her head. "But if that's all true about someone purposefully sending it over, how can we ever verify it?"

Professor Hudson shrugged. "Maybe, with enough time in the Great Library, we might find someone who talked about it in a brief footnote. But honestly, the fact that this thing exists is impressive enough. Not all mysteries need to be solved. Sometimes, their results are enough to bring satisfaction."

"I'm stunned," Professor Powell said. "Floored."

A huge grin split Cameron's face. "In other words, it's the ultimate survey finding."

"That it is," Professor Tarelli said with a nod.

Raine looked at the professors. "If we don't scare the animals or cause prolonged suffering, there'll be fewer earthquakes, right?"

Professor Powell nodded. "That would likely be the case."

"Then do we have to go?" She let the hope bleed into her voice.

"No, all we have to do is respect the island." He looked at Professor Hudson, who nodded calmly. "And if we do that, you could probably even play mazeball again." He grinned.

Raine lay back, her head swimming with all the information—an entire island that surrounded a gigantic long-lived creature that was to gnomes as gnomes were to normal humans. Every time she thought she had a handle on what it meant to be a witch in a world of magic, something new blindsided her and made her question everything.

And that was the most wonderful feeling in the world.

CHAPTER THIRTY

Her packing finished, Raine sighed and stretched. The last few weeks of the summer trip had gone without incident. As Professor Tarelli predicted, the earthquakes lessened, with only two minor tremors. Despite the fact that they hadn't ceased completely, they were small enough that the professors allowed the students to resume their mazeball.

The game was a fun distraction, although Adrien, Finn, Asher, and Philip all agreed that it needed too much refinement to be a sport played anywhere but on tiny islands during summer research trips.

Evie zipped her suitcase briskly. "I thought I would be happy to leave, but I'll miss this place. It almost feels like I'm leaving home, and it'll take me a few days to process how I feel about that."

Sara nodded from her bed. "I feel the same way."

"We played a part in history here," Raine said. "According to Professor Hudson, the US government and the UN are talking about how best to handle the island. It's obviously in American territory, but it's a unique lifeform on Earth, so everyone's concerned that it be protected in the best way possible." She laughed at a sudden realization.

"What's so funny?" The kitsune looked confused.

"I thought about how no one knows how to handle Madelyn because she's a too new type of life, and no one knows how to handle the mallaoch because it's too old." She smiled. "It's interesting, is all."

"Life always is," Sara said.

The ferry extended its ramp to the dock. Both groups of students had travelled from the island together and now disembarked in Portland. From there, they would take the Starbucks train to their hometowns. Even though they would go to the same transit location, everyone used the opportunity to say their final goodbyes on the ferry, since they didn't want to risk revealing the magic train. Someday, it might be a matter of public record but for now, it remained a semi-secret.

Raine shook Silas' hand. "It was nice getting to know you. Thanks for that list of books. I'll read all of them."

"It's always good to meet a fellow book lover." The boy smiled before he added a final shy nod and headed toward the ramp.

Finn fist-bumped Adrien. "Just so you know, bro, I won't show you any mercy on the Louper field. Once I put the uniform on, I'm loyal to my team first and everyone else second. Even my family!"

The Light Elf scoffed. "I would be insulted if you dared

to show me mercy. The best way to show your respect is by attempting to destroy me, as I will you when we go undefeated next season."

"Yeah, I'll personally make sure you have at least one loss next season." He grinned.

"We'll see." Adrien nodded and stepped away, a smile on his face.

Josephine left her suitcase and walked toward Sara to pull her into a tight hug. "It's been my greatest pleasure to spend these last two months with you, Sara. You're a wonderful person, and I loved your sketches. I hope I can see your paintings in person someday."

The kitsune hugged her affectionately. "You're great, too, Jo."

Evie came in for a hug with the witch. She'd finished her goodbyes with Heidi and Kelly. Tears ran down her reddened cheeks.

Cameron shook Asher's hand. "Go kick a few monster butts for me, or you could go a semester without getting wrapped up in some weird creature-related incident."

The Wood Elf grinned. "Same to you, Cameron. Try and avoid chaos witches for at least a few months or any killer game faeries who come to life. Heck, avoid any ferrets wearing fancy clothes too."

"I'll try but no promises." The shifter inclined his head toward Raine. "She ends up dragging me into any number of things, and I have to back my girlfriend, you know."

Asher's grin managed to somehow grow even bigger. "Oh, yeah. That I do know."

Dnai smiled bashfully at Asher from the ramp. She turned and stuck her hand over her mouth.

Cameron glanced from Asher to the Arpak girl. "What was that about? Wait. You and Dnai? I thought you weren't dating anyone from your school?"

"We're a thing now," his companion murmured with a shrug. "We always liked each other, but it never seemed to happen. But over those last few days on the island, I spent more time with her and we talked, and now, we'll make it work at school. It's not like we don't both already know one another. I always thought my first girlfriend would be an elf, but it's funny how life works out."

"It's good that you're together," the shifter said a little too forcefully. "Very good. I'm happy for you."

The Wood Elf smirked. "You want me away from Raine, huh?"

Cameron shrugged. "I won't say the thought never occurred to me."

"She is a special girl, Cameron. Don't ever let her go."

"I won't. I can guarantee that."

"Good." Asher gave him a little salute and turned away, a huge smile on his face. He headed toward Dnai and threw his arm over her shoulder.

Raine sighed quietly and stepped away from all the hugging and handshakes. While she would only be away from her Trouble Squad friends for a few weeks, the weight of the summer adventure pressed heavily on her. She approached the railing and looked at the water as she thought about how things had changed and how they had also stayed the same.

Professor Hudson stepped out of the passenger area. She closed the door quietly behind her and moved to the girl's side. "Is everything okay? You look somewhat pensive."

"It's great." Raine chuckled quietly. "Wonderful, actually. I'm eager to get back to FBI training, but we stopped poachers, I made new friends, and I helped discover a rare, ancient creature. It wasn't a bad summer when you think about it. And no one had to die."

"Cherish these days, Raine," the professor said gently. "Take joy in what it means to still be a young person experiencing so many of life's firsts. I know you're very eager to join the FBI, but you'll have more than enough time to be an adult. Make the most of your last year at the School of Necessary Magic."

"I know." She turned to gaze at everyone she'd shared the summer with. "Thank you, Professor, for giving us this opportunity. It was something I needed, but I didn't actually know I did. I don't think I'll forget this summer for the rest of my life." She wiped away a few tears that threatened at the corners of her eyes.

Professor Hudson patted her on the shoulder. "That's what we always strive to do as educators. Thank you for always being hungry for knowledge. Its students like you and your friends who refresh my love of teaching."

Raine drew a deep breath. "Um, I had a question. Is Madelyn…still at the school?"

"Yes. She will be a sophomore next year and treated like any other, despite her…exotic origin." The woman smiled warmly. "But I'm sure she could use a few upperclassmen friends, and maybe when she is a junior, she can have a wonderful summer trip as well that gives her great memories.

"That would be nice."

Professor Hudson rested a hand on the railing. "You really can't leave anyone alone when they're in trouble, can you?"

She chuckled. "No, I don't think I can."

"You only have one more year to get into trouble at our school. Make the best of it." Professor Hudson lowered her hand. "We'll see you soon, Raine. Enjoy the last few weeks of your summer."

"Thank you, Professor, I will."

Raine walked back toward the others and grinned. She would make the best of it. Uncle Jerry had already agreed to let Cameron spend the last weeks of summer at their house.

Summer might be ending, but the story is far from over. Raine's adventure continues in Probationary Agent.

FREE BOOKS!

WARNING:

The Troll is now in charge.

And he's giving away free books
- if you sign-up!

Join the only newsletter hosted by a Troll!

Get sneak peeks, exclusive giveaways, behind the scenes
content, and more.
PLUS you'll be notified of special **one day only fan
pricing** on new releases.

CLICK HERE

or visit: https://marthacarr.com/read-free-stories/

For Hire: Teachers for special school in Virginia countryside.

Must be able to handle teenagers with special abilities.

Cannot be afraid to discipline werewolves, wizards, elves and other assorted hormonal teens.

Apply at the School of Necessary Magic.

AVAILABLE ON AMAZON RETAILERS AND IN KINDLE UNLIMITED!

Find the compass, save the world or save herself?

Dating is harder for Maggie Parker than running down a felon. Now add in magic.

Did she just see a compass fly?

Can she learn how to use the magic of bubbles to chart a new course in time? It's a lot harder than it sounds.

Join her on her quest to rescue passengers on an ancient ship – a big blue marble called Earth – and save herself.

AVAILABLE ON AMAZON AND IN KINDLE UNLIMITED!

Make Your Own Mountain – it's a favorite saying of Michael Anderle's and for a long time I didn't really pay full attention to it. I was too busy climbing whatever mountain was in front of me. Besides, what does 'make your own mountain' even mean?

I can't make a mountain, can I?

But then success came, and I was able to lift my head and look around a little and even more interesting, I had choices to make. All good choices no less – but I still had to choose. Imagine if you're from a long line of hardworking people who did their best, went to a job, paid their bills, raised their kids, took vacations, went to family reunions, celebrated holidays, basically had a good life and then passed on to the next.

That's the storyline for generations behind me.

Now, what if you suddenly could pause, not work quite as hard, take more vacations, travel in style, live where you want and design your life – not just make the most out of what you have. That is suddenly me.

I heard the phrase again and in a flash, I got what he meant. Make Your Own Mountain means Make Your Own Dream, not someone else's. If you're striving for more because others have more, you haven't asked the right question yet. If you're dieting and exercising to get down to a certain size because that's what others say looks good, wrong question. (By the way, I've done both of those)

If you're doing anything because you're competing with yourself or others, the most important and powerful question is still missing.

What do you want? Answer that one and keep walking toward the answer and your own mountain will appear. That's the one to climb – but first you have to create it. Took me forever to have the courage to even ask myself the question, let alone wait for the answer. If someone asked, what do you want to do, I was more likely to answer with – I don't know, what do you want to do? Over time, I no longer knew, which means I didn't know myself.

Fortunately, I cut that out and started putting the pieces of my mountain together till one day I reached this peak of the very old mountain that was always right in front of me. So, I suppose this is part two and sometimes you have to create another mountain. Look at that – a mountain range in all new territory.

It's going to take a little time and some trust in the universe and in myself to ask the question again and wait for entirely new answers. If I'm not trying to make sure the basics are covered, if I have time to do other things – What do I want to do?

The first answer was to write The Peabrain Adventures – and frankly, to keep that name. You have to read the series to get why it matters to much. It's part of my new mountain – maybe the foothills or the first camp. The next may be to travel more – there's a lot in the US I've never seen. I've already got a trip planned to see Niagara Falls. Why not? And I keep adding places to the list. Santa Fe, Napa Valley, Glacier National Park (and glamping – it's a thing).

This is the beginning of the last great journey of my life. My last mountain. Definitely worthy of a few moments to answer that powerful question – what do I want? Stay tuned...

More adventures to follow.

THANK YOU for not only reading this story but these *Author Notes* **as well.**

(I think I've been good with always opening with "thank you." If not, I need to edit the other *Author Notes*!)

RANDOM (*sometimes***) THOUGHTS?**

The awesome of Indie Publishing.

Travel… It's 'mostly' awesome except when it isn't (fiery plane crashes anyone?)

We travel a lot for publishing (you don't have to, it is a strategic decision on my part to put LMBPN at all four of the major Book Fairs each year.) However, I can't say that having two plane crashes in the last few days has made me feel any safer about the trip part.

I'm REALLY ready for the transporter 'beam me to Beijing Scotty' option.

Only problem is I lose the reading time. I can be guaranteed that during take off and landing the only option I have to work is to read.

(Shhh, don't mention that I can type on my phone, give an older man a break, please?)

Oh yeahhhh... I know I look younger than my 51 years, but I'm going to start milking my age for all the benefits.

Like, napping because I'm over 50 (not because I stayed up until 4:30 reading that latest book last night... Stupid thing was LOOOONG and I wanted to see what happened to the characters.)

Or saying I have wisdom because of the gray hairs on my head. I know the hair is strictly because of my age, but I'm using that explanation forever.

Back to flying and travel, I digressed.

Essentially, I'm flying on purpose to build the company and help other indie authors around the world. So, I'm taking the risk. I suspect in another couple of years, I'll dial back on the travel (last time to Australia for at least a couple of years or longer.)

I'm happy to say I did an around the world trip (this summer) but man, I don't want to plan one again anytime soon.

Unless I get one of those apartment type rooms I hear about.

AROUND THE WORLD IN 80 DAYS

One of the interesting (at least to me) aspects of my life is the ability to work from anywhere and at any time. In the future, I hope to re-read my own *Author Notes* and remember my life as a diary entry.

Cave in the Sky (™) **Las Vegas, Nevada**

It's starting to get warm here in Las Vegas and I figure

the painful part of living in a desert is going to come too soon.

Personally, I wonder if in the future I'll re-read these author notes and still have this condo, or will we have sold it because of the weather?

Only time will tell.

FAN PRICING

$0.99 Saturdays (new LMBPN stuff) and $0.99 Wednesday (both LMBPN books and friends of LMBPN books.) Get great stuff from us and others at tantalizing prices.

Go ahead, I bet you can't read just one.

Sign up here: http://lmbpn.com/email/.

HOW TO MARKET FOR BOOKS YOU LOVE

Review them so others have your thoughts, tell friends and the dogs of your enemies (because who wants to talk with enemies?)... *Enough said ;-)*

Ad Aeternitatem,

Michael Anderle

OTHER SERIES IN THE ORICERAN
UNIVERSE:

SCHOOL OF NECESSARY MAGIC
SCHOOL OF NECESSARY MAGIC: RAINE CAMPBELL
ALISON BROWNSTONE
THE DANIEL CODEX SERIES
THE LEIRA CHRONICLES
I FEAR NO EVIL
FEDERAL AGENTS OF MAGIC
THE UNBELIEVABLE MR. BROWNSTONE
REWRITING JUSTICE
THE KACY CHRONICLES
MIDWEST MAGIC CHRONICLES
SOUL STONE MAGE
THE FAIRHAVEN CHRONICLES

OTHER BOOKS BY JUDITH BERENS

OTHER BOOKS BY MARTHA CARR

JOIN THE ORICERAN UNIVERSE FAN GROUP ON FACEBOOK!

BOOKS BY MICHAEL ANDERLE

For a complete list of books by Michael Anderle, please visit

www.lmbpn.com/ma-books/

All LMBPN Audiobooks are Available at Audible.com and
iTunes. For a complete list of audiobooks visit:

www.lmbpn.com/audible

CONNECT WITH THE AUTHORS

Martha Carr Social

Website: http://www.marthacarr.com

Facebook: https://www.facebook.com/
groups/MarthaCarrFans/

Michael Anderle Social

Michael Anderle Social
Website:
http://www.lmbpn.com

Email List:
http://lmbpn.com/email/

Facebook Here: https://www.
facebook.com/TheKurtherianGambitBooks/